Pearl

in the

Rice

Father Leo Booth
with Kien Lam

Long Beach, California
SCP Limited
2003

Pearl in the Rice

Father Leo Booth
with Kien Lam

Published by: SCP Limited
2105 East 27th Street
Signal Hill, CA 90755

This book is manufactured in the United States of America.

ISBN 1-892841-05-3

Contents

Acknowledgments

$\mathcal{P}$ earl in the Rice did not just happen. It was born out of the imagination and hard work of the following people:

Kien Lam. He had the original idea. He held the dream. And he was also the sole translator of the book from Vietnamese into English. Because he is my office manager, that meant working at home until late at night, choosing the right word or phrase to reflect exactly what was said in the stories he grew up with. It was challenging work.

"Leo, my head aches. Will it ever end?" was sometimes Kien's lament, but in actuality, he devoted himself to the project with unfaltering dedication and genuine love. And, yes, it did end. His hard work has paid off. Kien selected the endearing stories you will now be able to enjoy in English, having preserved the Vietnamese flavor of the original narratives. Bravo!

Cynthia Cavalcanti. No writer can survive without an exceptional editor. Sometimes gently, and more often firmly, Cynthia urged Kien and me to complete the collection and translation of the stories, eager to get her hands on them and work her magic.

I am honored Cynthia was involved in this project because she brings a deep spiritual perspective to her work and immediately embraced the meaning of this collection from a soul place.

Anna Woo. Anna worked diligently to create a cover for the book that captures the essence of the stories inside. Her design is not only Asian, or Eastern, but decidedly Vietnamese, with the right color coordination. Obviously, a book is more than its cover, but the cover is the first thing you see. Anna has done a fabulous job.

And I would like to thank you, the reader. A book is written so it can be read. Without you, a key ingredient would be missing. I know you will enjoy. And, as with all wisdom, please pass it on.

I am blessed to spend so much of my time surrounded by positive and creative people. It makes a big difference to the living of my life. Now, I have been able to reach into one of the most ancient cultures in Asia and bring to you the pearl that has for so long been hidden in the rice.

Leo Booth

Pearl

in the

Rice

Introduction
Lời Giới Thiệu

$\mathcal{K}$ien Lam, my dear friend and office manager, came to me four years ago with an idea: "Leo, why don't I translate some beautiful Vietnamese fables into English for you to write up into a book? Believe me, these stories are so spiritual and filled with ancient wisdom. Your people would love them!"

And so was the birth of Pearl in the Rice.

It took four years to select the right stories for people who are in recovery or searching for spiritual wisdom in the ordinary things of life. Continuing my spiritual theme that began over 20 years ago, I am proud of these transforming fables written in a simple style that appeals to children and adults alike.

These stories are special. Largely unknown to Western audiences, they explore the major themes all of us face in our daily lives and, through rich narrative and vivid symbolism, show us how to confront those challenges effectively, from a place of love. In addition, they have a Vietnamese flavor that reflects the personality of the people–endearing, sensitive, gentle, and simple, yet delightfully colorful.

Each of the stories is unique, a fresh rendition of time-honored values woven into a delightful tale. Let me offer you a brief synopsis of what you will discover inside:

Snake Head
We receive spiritual rewards for the compassion we demonstrate in our lives. A blessing cannot accommodate greed.

Little Princess and Blind Horse
This fable explores the spiritual value of personal independence. Often, we already know intuitively what is right for us.

The Blessing Bridge
Real change requires decision and dedicated work. The rewards are infinite.

Born Again as a Hen
The spiritual life avoids wastefulness. Here, we learn to discover God in the small things.

The Monk and His Disciple
If we look through the eyes of God, we see beauty in everything. Spirituality is based on embracing life, not avoiding it.

Tiger and Little Toad
Here we see the gentle victory of innocence over bullying. Success often involves ingenuity, taking risks, and perhaps being a little crafty.

Hunter
Balance and respect are ingredients in the good life. Instinct is seen as a key to spiritual connection. Willful killing destroys us all.

Golden Hole or Silver Hole
If we are too greedy, we only inherit tragedy. We must trust in divine process and wisdom.

Red Rat with Bulging Eyes
Real beauty is often discovered behind the outer appearance. Only by living the good life do we discover peace and happiness.

Lazy Man
Indolence eventually leads to unhappiness. Divine Spirit expects us to actively create our personal peace and prosperity, and in doing so, we receive the best.

King Magpie
True relationships are based on soul connections. Sometimes, we have to break a few clay pots to heal a heart.

Best Friends
Innocence often precedes tragedy. However, miracles do happen if you are persistent.

Through these stories, we realize the Pearl, or wisdom, is always waiting to be revealed in the everyday, ordinary events of life, i.e., the Rice. This book honors the genuine beauty of spirituality passed on from an ancient culture in another time to us–the spiritual seekers of today. Discover Pearl in the Rice.

Snake Head
Đầu Rắn

Somewhere in a distant land, a young married couple gave birth to three handsome sons. Each son had his own distinct personality and disposition.

The oldest son was very critical.

The middle son was haughty and uptight.

The youngest son was kind, gentle, and friendly to everyone.

As the years passed by and the three brothers grew up, the time came for the mother and father to sit down with their sons and prepare them for a life on their own.

"You are all growing up nicely, and we would like each of you to find a beautiful girl to love, so you can marry and have children of your own. Besides, you are all at an age when you can play a vital role in the family business. The time has come for you to go into the city buying and selling fabrics and silks. If you remember to be considerate in your bartering, you will return home with a healthy profit.

"We will help you become responsible businessmen by dividing the family gold and silver equally between the three of you. We will also give you a horse you can use to carry the delicate fabrics to sell in the marketplace. All these things we give you because we love you very much."

So the three brothers set off to begin a life of family responsibility, trading fabrics and silks in the marketplace. They became extremely successful.

Truth be told, it was the oldest brother and middle brother who exceeded in selling and trading the fabrics; the youngest brother did not seem interested in business. He was absorbed in studying ancient herbal medicines and special ointments that could be developed through the prayers and experiences of the holy men in the city. His older brothers criticized him on a regular basis, but the younger brother was determined to learn all he could from the holy men, and he did not change his ways.

One day, the three brothers set off for the city and midway along their journey, they came upon a lush forest and decided to rest in the shade under the trees. The youngest brother fell into a deep sleep from which his older brothers could not wake him. After a while, they left him sleeping and went on into the city to sell and trade their delicate fabrics.

Eventually, the younger brother woke up because he rarely slept for very long. As he freshened himself up at a nearby stream, he saw a snake (*con rắn*) on the pathway.

"Please help me," cried the snake. "My skin is dried up by the hot rays of the sun. It is blistering terribly, and I fear if I do not get help soon, I will surely die."

As he listened to the snake with pity in his heart, the young brother looked up and saw a lizard resting on a leaf he recognized from his studies with the holy men. He knew this precious leaf contained healing properties.

The lizard sensed the young brother would require use of the leaf he was resting upon and slowly crawled under the shade of a tender eucalyptus tree.

The lizard was not especially fond of the snake. As you may know, snakes and lizards only tolerate each other, rarely becoming good friends.

However, from within the shade of the eucalyptus, the lizard uttered these prophetic words: "You are a holy young man. You seek to heal creatures that are in distress or pain. This action will lead to great rewards."

The lizard then closed his eyes. It is hard to know whether he was sleeping or not, because lizards often close their eyes for long periods of time for no apparent reason.

The young brother used the precious leaf to gently stroke the sick snake. The healing oils from the leaf were absorbed into the snake's skin, and eventually, the snake began to heal. Soon, the snake was looking more like his moist and slippery self.

"Your kindness has not gone unnoticed, for kindness is a sacred quality." Then the snake slipped past the lizard into the shade. The lizard did not bother to open his eyes. Perhaps he was really sleeping.

After the snake had healed and moved away, the two older brothers returned, laden with expensive silks and fabrics. Seeing their younger brother kneeling beside the stream, they scolded him for going into a deep sleep and not joining them with their business in the city.

The young brother told them about the dried up snake that was in need of healing, but they were unconcerned. They did not like healthy snakes, so they were certainly not interested in a sick snake!

"You have not helped us sell and barter in the city. You have no silks to take back to mother and father. They will be angry with you when they see you come home empty-handed. Helping sick snakes is a waste of time and energy. Playing with sacred ointments will never make you rich and powerful. Look at the holy men in the city. They are holy and poor!"

The two brothers walked away, leaving their younger brother crying in the forest. They took the horse and fabrics with them, and the poor little brother was left all alone.

After he cried and felt depressed, the sun began to set and the young brother decided it was time to journey home. As he traveled along the dusty pathway, he came across a tiny hamlet with only maybe three or four houses. It was just beyond the forest. He noticed a small group of children had formed a circle and were beating something with sticks. Echoing within the boys' shouts of glee was a piercing cry of pain. What could the children be striking?

When he moved closer, he saw that the children had beaten a snake to death. They had crushed its body and severed its head. When the children saw the young brother coming toward them, they ran away; like most gangs, they were connected to each other by the thread of cowardice and shame.

The younger brother looked at the snake, again, with pity in his heart. Then, he remembered the precious leaf with its healing oils and he immediately ran back to find the leaf, close to where the lizard had been resting in the shade of the tender eucalyptus tree.

The lizard had remained in the shade and had since been joined by another lizard. They both seemed to enjoy each other's company as they rested alongside each other with their eyes shut. The leaf was close to where it had been left.

The young brother brought the leaf to the wounded snake and placed it around his severed head, which had been pulled away from his mutilated body.

It looked very strange to see a snake head separated from a snake body, even stranger to wrap a leaf around a little snake head. However, the healing began almost immediately and, strangely enough, the snake head smiled!

It was at this moment that the young brother recognized the snake he had healed earlier near the river was the same snake that had been beaten by the naughty children with sticks. He recognized the snake smile. It was a beautiful smile because it revealed a gentle love.

Then, the snake head spoke. "First, you healed me. And now, you have brought me back to life with the same precious leaf. Your acts of kindness have not gone unnoticed.

"You are such a wonderful young man. You rescued my poor little head from the naughty children. I am so grateful to you. Now the time has come for you to receive. This is the best way to create harmony (thịnh vượng) in life. You do a kindness to me, and then I do a kindness.

"I have a special blessing for you. Would you like it?"

"What is it?" asked the young brother. He was always pleased to accept a blessing.

"Well," continued the snake, "you must put my little head in your pocket and when you need anything, you say aloud, 'Snake Head, Snake Head, Snake Head,' three times. You must say it three times. If you only say it once or twice, it will not work. Blessings are like that–if you do not get the formula exactly right, they will not work. So, remember to say, 'Snake Head' three times. Then, what you wish for will be granted to you."

The young brother nodded his head, signifying that he understood. His father had often told him when they visited the Temple together that blessings can be funny things. If you do not get the formula exactly right, they will not work. Indeed, they can sometimes become a curse. And nobody wants that.

So the young brother put Snake Head in his pocket. He began the long journey home.

As he walked, he became very tired. He felt weak. He had to sit down. With the tiredness came a sadness. He began to cry. Then, he suddenly remembered Snake Head in his pocket.

He pulled it out and repeated three times, "Snake Head, Snake Head, Snake Head." As he said those words, he wished for a horse to carry him home.

Suddenly, a white horse appeared before him. It was very beautiful–more beautiful than the one his parents had given him and his brothers. It came with a decorous gold riding seat.

Also, neatly packed on either side of the horse were two baskets of elegant fabrics and silks. Now he not only had a beautiful horse, but expensive merchandise to make his mother and father very happy.

He arrived at the family home very late. It was after midnight. He said to himself, "I will not disturb my parents. They are sleeping. I know what I will do. I will ask Snake Head for shelter."

So he pulled Snake Head from his pocket and said three times, "Snake Head, Snake Head, Snake Head." As he did so, he wished for shelter and maybe a little food, for the younger brother was never greedy.

Suddenly, there appeared a beautiful house with servants going in and out, singing as they went. On an open fire, he could see a chicken being cooked. Also, mangoes and wine were already placed on the table.

He looked down at Snake Head and smiled. The younger brother was always polite and well mannered.

When morning came, the parents were delighted to see their youngest son return with the beautiful house and singing servants. They gently jumped for joy when they saw the beautiful white horse laden with elegant fabrics and silks.

In fact, the parents did a little dance that made the younger brother smile. It was a short dance, because the parents were quite old!

"Now we can all live together with delicious food and singing servants," said the younger brother.

"You are such a good son," said Father. Mother smiled in agreement.

The younger brother sat down and told his parents about the healing leaf oil and the blessings he had received from Snake Head. As he recounted the story, he pulled Snake Head out of his pocket and showed it to the parents.

The parents smiled. Snake Head smiled back. They were all very happy.

Eventually, the older brother and middle brother heard about Snake Head and asked if they could borrow it. The younger brother was reluctant, because he knew it was a sacred blessing *(phúc đức)* Snake Head had given to him and him alone.

However, he loved his brothers and wanted everybody to be happy. So he allowed his brothers to borrow Snake Head.

They did exactly what the younger brother told them, saying, "Snake Head, Snake Head, Snake Head." Three times. As they spoke, they wished for gold and silver.

Suddenly, the brothers were surrounded by bags of gold and silver. Now everybody was rich. They had, overnight, become the wealthiest family in the village.

But the brothers were very greedy. Unlike the younger brother, who never asked for too much and always shared with family and friends, the two older brothers always wanted more. They both kept shouting, "Snake Head, Snake Head, Snake Head," non-stop in a very angry tone.

Poor little Snake Head became afraid. Then he got dizzy. He was working too hard trying to give the two brothers what they wanted, but it was never enough. They just kept yelling, "Snake Head, Snake Head, Snake Head" in a nasty voice that reminded him of the naughty children from the hamlet who had beaten him with sticks.

Snake Head could not stand the noise anymore. He jumped up and bit the two brothers. They died immediately, surrounded by the bags of silver and gold.

The younger brother picked up Snake Head, stroking the top of his head as he did so. Snake Head was still confused and a little dizzy.

The parents, the singing servants, and the village neighbors smiled at Snake Head because they knew he had been pushed beyond the normal expectations any snake, let alone a little Snake Head, could be expected to endure. As Snake Head basked in the smiles of the young brother, the parents, the singing servants, and the neighbors, he felt loved again. The young brother gently returned Snake Head to his pocket where he had always felt safe and cozy.

It was sad to see the two brothers lying dead on the ground, surrounded by their bags of silver and gold. However, the younger brother, the parents, the singing servants, and the neighbors all knew that a blessing can never accommodate greed.

Little Princess and Blind Horse
Công Chúa Nhỏ và con Ngựa Mù

In ancient times, there was a King who had three daughters. All three Princesses were beautiful. However, the two older sisters were united in the belief that it was the duty of their future husbands to take care of them, meaning they would live off the wealth and power each husband possessed.

For this reason, when the time came for them to pick husbands, their main consideration was which man in the kingdom had enormous gold reserves, land, property, and all the trappings that come with such riches. Thus, they married into a luxurious lifestyle, everyday eating at sumptuous banquets, playing in beautifully manicured gardens, and generally spending their days in idle gossip.

23

Neither Princess gave a thought to lifting a finger to do any work because they each had servants to take care of their every whim. They were both equally spoiled, and they loved every minute of it.

The youngest Princess, whom everyone at the Palace called "Little Princess" *(công chúa nhỏ)* because she was tiny in stature, felt differently about life and love. From a very young age, she had an independent streak and grew up never wanting to live off anyone. She feared that marrying into wealth would make her lazy and dependent on the good fortune of others.

Little Princess had a mind of her own and was determined to take care of herself. She also had a romantic dream: finding a loving companion who was equally independent in spirit so they could be successful together and build up their own fortune.

Once, the King tried to encourage Little Princess to marry the son of the Prime Minister, who belonged to a noble and wealthy family in the region. She emphatically declined because although he was both noble and wealthy, the son was cruel and unkind to many people living in the Palace.

Behind his back, the servants called him Crow Face because he was so disrespectful and mean. Little Princess could never marry such a man.

After hearing the Princess' protestations against marrying the Prime Minister's son, the King was angry and had to be calmed down by the Queen, who took him into the garden to observe the beautiful peacocks and gave him oranges *(trái cam)* to eat. Most times, these little excursions did the trick, and the Queen gently reminded the King not to force Little Princess into marriage.

Some time later, a high-ranking officer, possibly equal to a general in today's army, proposed an arranged marriage between his son and the independent Princess.

Still, Little Princess refused and said sweetly to her father, "Dearest Father, I know this young man is the son of your most famous military officer with much power and influence in your kingdom, but truly he is a useless man. He is incompetent, lazy, and lacking in the most basic of skills.

"All day long, he spends his time drinking and partying with the other parasites that roam this Palace. Father, if you care for my life, you could not, should not, ask me to marry this man."

The King became uncontrollable in his anger and the Queen was not around to take him into the garden and feed him oranges. His face became purple with rage as he blurted out to his daughter, "You are very stupid. Not only stupid, but crazy in your low-class desire to find true love at the expense of wealth and security. Why can't you be more like your sisters?"

Little Princess remained quiet and respectful in the face of her father's tirade, knowing deep in her heart that the King only wanted what he thought was best for her, even though he was wrong. So very, very wrong.

Angrily, the King continued, "You have refused the two most appropriate and wealthy suitors in my kingdom. You have disgraced my status as King. You are behaving like a romantic wench from any tavern in my kingdom. You are a fool–and a stupid fool at that!"

Calmly, yet firmly, Little Princess said, "Father, is it so wrong to want to earn my own wealth? Is it so wrong to want to earn whatever possessions I might create? Why must I find security and happiness in the luxury of another?"

Then she said it. Never had it been said before, but every citizen knew it to be true: "Your grandfather began from nothing."

The King could hardly contain himself. "Grandfather was a man. Men create wealth. Women are created to adorn and enhance the wealth of their husbands."

"Like a peacock," she muttered.

"I heard you. Yes, like a peacock–I mean a peahen." The poor King did not quite know what he was saying, but he knew it was true because he was King.

He called his servants to bring out the skinny, blind horse that was years past its prime. He had, in previous years, wanted the horse butchered and served to the poor, but the Queen had yet again intervened with a walk in the garden and a basket of oranges. However, the Queen was still nowhere to be seen.

"Here is my gift to you, ungrateful daughter, this skinny, blind horse. You turn your back on luxury and power. You refuse to marry the noble men I bring before you. Now seek your destiny among the poor. Take your independent spirit and make your wealth from the dirt. Do not contact me again until you can prove your success."

Strangely, Little Princess was not sad. Rather, she was excited at the chance to prove herself and with her own endeavors make something of her life. Secretly, this was what she had been praying for to the Buddha *(Phật)*.

Gathering a few belongings, she took the reins of the skinny, blind horse, first caressing his head in her gentle hands saying, "Horsey, my sweet horsey, you are my new friend. Already I love you, and I know our adventure together will be most successful. Lord Buddha walks with us. Do not be afraid."

The blind horse gently nudged her with his head. It was an example of horse love. Little Princess understood.

"One day, my blind friend, we will be rich and happy. Secure in a love that is both noble and true. How? When? Today, I do not have the answers to those questions. But I know that although you are blind, you will lead me to my destiny.

"This I believe. And this I know. Some years ago, I was told by a spiritual master, 'A blind horse shall lead you.' At the time, I did not understand. Today, I have discovered trust and faith."

The blind horse nudged her more enthusiastically.

"Yes, my friend. It is all very exciting. You will lead me to happiness. You will lead me to my true love. But I will never forget you, and so I promise I will find a healer who will cure your blindness. Today you are blind, but soon you will see again.

"Now lead the way. My future lies in each step you take."

The skinny, blind horse gave a few gentle whinnies that indicated it was time to go. Darkness was approaching.

The blind horse knew they had many miles to travel. Little Princess elegantly mounted the blind horse and they set off from the Palace on their journey with their heads held high.

The Queen passed by them at the Palace gate and waved. She was carrying a basket of oranges for the King!

They traveled many miles beyond the Palace, but Little Princess felt secure in the knowledge that wherever the blind horse went, so it was meant to be. Blind Horse was strong and firm in his steps, walking along the rocky paths as if knowing every twist and turn; it was as if he were miraculously being led.

Blind Horse passed through villages, towns, and small hamlet communities, plodding up mountain terrain and crossing rushing rivers. Little Princess felt safe, carrying excitement and expectation in her heart.

They passed temples, mansions, and luxurious homes, but Blind Horse did not stop. He kept moving ahead with his ears standing straight and his eyes fixed with a knowing blindness.

Some time later, if only for a few moments, Little Princess entertained a worry. "Perhaps he is lost. It seems as if we have passed everything. There are no more lights, and the darkness is making my eyes dim."

But Blind Horse continued. Resolute. Committed to each step he made. Little Princess cast aside her doubts and fears. Intuitively, she sensed he knew where he was going.

Blind Horse stopped outside a small wooden cottage next to a beautiful, rippling stream. Although it was dark, Little Princess could see wildflowers in all directions.

Blind Horse whinnied an affirming tone and swung his neck with definite nods as if to say, "We are here. We have arrived."

An old lady and her handsome son stepped out of the cottage door to greet them. Little Princess soon learned the woman was a widow.

Her son worked diligently each day in the local coal mine and sold the coal at the local market. The village people called him Coal Burner, because he delivered the coal they bought to burn in their homes.

Mother and son graciously asked Little Princess to come into their humble cottage and eat some freshly prepared vegetables and rice. The princess knew she had arrived at the right place.

During the evening, Little Princess decided to tell them her story; how she had not wanted to marry into wealth, her constant arguments with the King, and her eventual banishment with the skinny, blind horse to find her true destiny.

"I believe it is my fate to be here!" The old lady immediately felt fear. How could the mother of Coal Burner entertain a princess?

Lowly people like herself did not mix with royalty. Her son, although strongly attracted to Little Princess, felt the same.

Bowing in humble obeisance before Little Princess, the old lady began to speak. "Your Royal Highness, as you can see, we are humble folk, not fit to be in the presence of the King's daughter. We entertain only village people. So with sincere respect, we feel completely embarrassed to have you stay with us. Please remain the evening in our humble abode, take your rest, and in the morning my son will escort you to the path that will enable you to continue your journey."

Little Princess listened to the old lady with a gentle spirit, but she was determined in her response. "My dearest lady, your heart is humble and kind. It is wonderful that you open your hospitality to me, feeding and watering my blind horse, but it is my fate to be with you. I know this in my heart.

"When I saw your son coming out to greet me earlier this evening, I sensed that he is the one I am to marry. Now I am even more convinced. I also know he has the same feelings for me."

Although Coal Burner felt nervous in the presence of a princess, it was undeniably true that he found the princess extremely beautiful. He felt the stirrings of love in his heart. As the princess spoke, he reached for the hand of his mother, nodding in agreement with Little Princess as he did so.

Little Princess continued, "Please let me be your daughter-in-law. Together, we will build a prosperous and beautiful life."

The old lady and Little Princess continued to talk throughout the night with Coal Burner nodding even more enthusiastically when the word "wedding" was mentioned. Finally, the old lady agreed.

Within days, the wedding took place. A local monk *(Sư Thầy)* was asked to perform the blessing, and the young couple promised to be faithful, living a joyous, loving, and productive life under God.

As the months passed, it became clear that Little Princess not only had a profound affection for Blind Horse, but for all horses. She had a natural instinct for these proud animals and soon became the most famous breeder and horse trainer in the kingdom. As she had invested her trust in Blind Horse, so now she invested her creativity in a horse farm and soon built up a thriving business.

Little Princess never neglected Blind Horse, her faithful friend. Each day she took care of him, taking him on walks in the hills beyond the coal mine and beside the rippling stream that fed the wildflowers near their cottage.

She would stop by a stream to give him a refreshing drink and occasionally a bath. Everyone who saw them on their rides sensed their happiness.

During one of their excursions in the hills, they met the Master who had performed her wedding. He was a powerful Buddhist teacher and healer, respected throughout the land. They talked as he gently stroked Blind Horse.

In his touch, the Master sensed the sickness that had made Blind Horse blind. Blind Horse was healthy and beautiful in every way, but the Master knew the root of the blindness. He also knew the cure.

Little Princess looked intently at Master. "Can you heal him?"

"Yes," said Master. "But you must go to Angel Mountain. Only there will you find the *mån tiá* leaves that have the healing properties for this kind of blindness. You must feed Blind Horse these leaves. Also, for three months you must give him the crystal-clear water that only flows down the rocks on Angel Mountain. If you promise to do this, Blind Horse will be healed."

Little Princess was elated. The promise she had made to Blind Horse when they first met was now coming true.

Each day for three months, she rode Blind Horse to Angel Mountain and fed him healing *mån tiá* leaves, followed by a bucket of crystal-clear, healing water. Each day, Blind Horse's sight slowly improved.

After the three months passed, according to the instructions of the Master, Blind Horse could see. Little Princess could hardly contain herself and danced for joy with her gentle, loving mother-in-law. Her husband laughed with the deep satisfaction of knowing all was well.

Permission was given by Little Princess for all the children in the village to ride Blind Horse. This made him feel both special and useful. He was often heard to make loud whinnies in the market square and was seen to be rolling his head with joy.

Occasionally, he danced a jig, but that was only on Holy Days. With great affection, all the villagers, including Little Princess, continued to call him Blind Horse.

Their lives continued to be happy and productive. Each day, Little Princess was seen walking Blind Horse in the hills surrounded by wildflowers or training her horses and teaching riding lessons to the village people. Her life was all she could have wished.

Amazing fortune also came to Coal Burner. One day, he discovered a new coal mine on Angel Mountain, but this coal mine was also mixed with traces of gold. Now, he mined not only coal, but also gold. Soon, he became one of the richest men in the kingdom. Some secretly said he was richer than the King!

Little Princess and Coal Burner shared some of their wealth with the local people, building a healing shrine next to the temple where the Master lived and prayed. They also built for themselves a beautiful marble palace, employing the best team of masons and architects in the kingdom.

Carpets, furniture, lamps, and gold goblets, embedded with precious gems, were brought in from every part of the kingdom. It was whispered to be more ornate and impressive than the King's Palace.

The time came for Little Princess and Coal Burner to invite the King and Queen to a Banquet of Reconciliation. Remember, the King had left Little Princess with the angry admonishment, "Do not contact me again until you can prove your success." Well, that time had come.

The King and Queen arrived to see the most beautifully constructed palace, manicured gardens inhabited by decorative peacocks, and the most impressive vision of gently swaying wildflowers. Proud, graceful horses cantered in the surrounding fields, and in the center was Blind Horse, playing with and carrying the village children. It was a picture of paradise.

The King and Queen greeted the beautiful and elegantly dressed Little Princess and her husband. The two mothers-in-law embraced. The King took Little Princess aside, with happy tears in his eyes, and gave her the longest of hugs. The royal family was reunited.

Close to the Queen, a servant was seen holding a basket of oranges.

The Blessing Bridge
Cái Cầu Phúc Đức

Long ago, there was a thief *(Kẻ trộm)* who practiced every day to improve his thieving skills. He lived on whatever he could steal. This was his way of life.

He had an elderly mother whom he needed to take care of because money was hard to come by, so he continued to do what he did so well–steal. To his way of thinking, it was the life the Buddha had dealt him.

He had perfected the art of breaking into people's houses in different ways, and some days, he was able to steal valuable objects that he would later sell in the city. But, of course, there were times when he broke into a home and found nothing.

41

Unfortunately, both mother and son were living a life without any real security for tomorrow.

One day, as was the custom in ancient times, and is still the custom today, he and his mother were celebrating the anniversary of his father's death *(giố ba)*. Sitting in a room filled with incense that accompanied the prayers said on this special day, his mother shared past memories of both his father and grandfather. The thief listened to his mother with rapt attention.

"Dear son, your grandfather was renowned throughout the land for being the most famous professional thief. Some nights, he was able to steal valuable objects that were worth a fortune, but his life was easy come, easy go. He spent as quickly as he stole. In old age, he died with his eyes closed, arms folded on his stomach, owning nothing. He was a pauper, leaving nothing for your father and me.

"Your father, growing up the son of such a thief, knew nothing of morality or personal respect. He only knew how to live from one day to the next–thieving. And like his father, your grandfather, there were nights when he was able to steal something of value that enabled him to survive, but there were many nights when he broke into a home and found nothing to steal. An empty-handed thief lives a tragic life!

"In old age, your father's life became sadder because he developed weak arms, crippled feet, and poor eyesight–even in the daytime. He became a crippled, blind, and slow-footed thief. He was hardly able to steal anything!

"Things were very difficult, my son, for both of us. Your father, in old age, had to depend on me. And we only survived by growing vegetables and raising chickens. But it was not enough. I was the wife of a poor thief, and when your father died, I had to sell the land to pay for the funeral."

As the thief listened to his mother recount the history of his grandfather and his father, it was like a mirror reflecting his own life. He saw his destiny laid out before him and knew that unless he changed his thieving ways, he would come to a tragic end.

But how do you stop stealing when it has been your way of life since you were a boy? How do you stop living a despised profession that has been in your family for two generations? The son went to bed sad and depressed with an empty tummy.

One night, the thief planned to steal from the Master Teacher who lived in the village. A group of students who stayed at Master's house had bought a roasted pig they intended to share with Master as a token of their appreciation for all he had done for them.

The thief intended to steal the roasted pig after they had all gone to sleep. But Master's candle was still burning after midnight, and the thief hid behind the door and listened to Master reading aloud from some sacred texts. *"All people should practice the spiritual sacredness of kindness. When they die, their honor continues to shine in a darkened world. If people follow the steps of the unkind, then the shadow of unkindness shall forever follow them.*

"Life is the time to decide. So many good and bad examples surround us. A person must learn the true example to follow."

Master Teacher then read a text from the Buddha. *"I am the Buddha who is. You are the Buddha who is becoming. Learn from the lotus flower I am sitting upon. It is the symbol of life's struggle. Within the lotus flower is its light and revealed beauty.*

"Remember that the lotus flower grows from the ground of mud. It struggles to be seen, growing through the mud and stinking water. Then it surfaces to face the sun in all its beauty."

As the thief listened to these words read aloud by Master Teacher, they were like arrows striking his heart and brain. It was as if his whole body was painfully spinning around to face a new reality.

He told himself, "Isn't it true that my father and grandfather spent their lives doing unkind deeds? I am suffering under the burden of their misdeeds. And only I can change my fate."

He ran from Master's house, through the forest of trees and streams where everything seemed so very dark and cold. Only the little light of hope he carried in his heart continued to shine.

He eventually found himself at home, and his mother was waiting for him with a warm cup of goat's milk. He shared with his mother all he had overheard from the Master Teacher and solemnly declared, "I will no longer steal other people's goods that they have worked hard to acquire. Instead, I will work hard with my own hands to establish my life, basing my future decisions on honesty and dignity."

The next morning, he went into the forest to chop wood so he could sell the product in the market for a few coins. The work was hard, and he could only sell enough wood to buy a bowl of rice, but at least he knew it was honest work.

Compared to his former life of stealing, when he was always anxious about being caught, he now relaxed knowing his soul was at peace. He went to bed with a smile on his face after sharing the bowl of rice with his mother.

But people in the marketplace were wary of him, saying, "Here comes the thief. The third generation of stealing is heading our way!"

This made the thief very sad. "One day, I will do something very good for all the people to see. It will bring a blessing on my family and the next generation will be respected. I shall trade in my past sins for the life of a decent man."

One hot summer day, a strange thing occurred with the weather. Although the sun was still shining, it rained and rained for many hours, and the stream near the village grew into a raging river.

Normally, the thief was able to jump across the stream to sell the wood he had chopped that morning, but now nobody could cross the rushing waters, and there was no ferryboat. Indeed, in the history of the village, a ferryboat had never been needed to cross the stream.

Many hundreds of people were now stranded on the other side of the river, unable to return to their homes and village.

Suddenly, the thief thought to himself, "Dear God, this is a serious problem for the people of the village. At any time, rains could come and make our little stream a raging river. We need a bridge.

"With your help, Great Buddha, I shall build a bridge for the people. They will no longer be stranded from their families. I shall do this great and noble thing, pay for my past sins as a thief, and also bring dignity and respect to my family name."

The thief wasted no time, and although many people had to sleep on the other side of the raging river, he spent his time telling the elders of the village they needed to build a strong bridge. The elders agreed.

"We recognize that our village needs a bridge for the future. It was attempted many years ago, but never completed. If you are able to build such a bridge, we are all willing to help in any way. Then, you will be a hero, and your family name will be blessed for generations to come."

The next morning, the river began to subside, and the stranded people wearily returned to their homes, soaking wet but safe. However, the thief had not lost his vision, and he shared with his mother his ideas about building a bridge for the village.

His mother was so very pleased to see her son's enthusiasm and told him not to worry about the household needs because she would take care of them. All he needed to do was concentrate his energies on building a beautiful bridge for the village.

The thief earnestly focused on the project of building a bridge. He spent the mornings developing his architectural plans for the construction, and in the afternoons, he went into the woods to select the right trees, by height and strength, for the necessary timber to build the bridge.

Also, he did not forget the little business he was developing; the small branches that were not needed for the bridge he saved and cut up to sell in the marketplace.

Day after day, night after night, and month after month, the thief devoted himself to the building of the bridge, spending every moment organizing the people of the village in the construction. They all grew to respect his hard work and prudent ideas in the building of this most necessary project.

But the hard work began to take its toll on the thief. Remember, most days he had only been eating rice and a little chicken.

Every day for weeks, the thief had been working on the building, making plans, cutting trees, and building heavy supports for the bridge. Eventually, he collapsed. All the people tried to comfort him, but he was exhausted.

At this time, a *Viên Quan* (a Mandarin officer), riding by on a horse, saw the commotion and asked what was wrong. The people explained, "This is the third generation of thievery who is seeking to wash away his family disgrace by doing a good and noble thing–building a bridge for the village. The people are already calling it 'the Blessing Bridge.' However, the thief has been working too hard and he collapsed because of exhaustion."

The *Viên Quan* took from his bag some special medicine and made the thief swallow it. After a while, the thief's energy rekindled and he returned to consciousness. The people were relieved and slowly drifted off to their homes.

The two were left alone. The *Viên Quan* wished to know more, and the thief felt comfortable in the presence of his new friend. "I am working hard to reclaim the honor for my family name. My father, my grandfather, and I have all been thieves, but I now wish to change my destiny and become a good and noble man. This village needs a strong bridge, and I am determined to build it, with the help of the people."

The *Viên Quan* listened carefully to all the thief said. Then, with a gentle and cultured voice, he spoke: "Your grandfather and your father did many dishonest things to the people. They were not spiritual role models for you to follow.

It is for this reason you were often sad, poor, and hungry, but you have found courage to choose a different path, a noble path. What you have chosen is a powerful goal, and future generations will call you a hero."

The *Viên Quan* was silent for a moment, then continued, "I need to tell you something about my family. My father, grandfather, and great grandfather all had important imperial positions throughout the kingdom, but each one, in different ways, abused his position. They mistreated the citizens, forced them to mine silver and gold for a pittance, and exploited the women and children–all for greed and power.

"So you see I, too, must make amends for my ancestors. I also need to reclaim honor for my family name. My life has been cursed because of their abuse. Can you believe I have been married for 20 years, and my wife and I are unable to have a child? We both feel this loss and live in a sad and lonely marriage. I also wish to do something noble to repay the sins of my family.

"Will you be kind enough to let me work with you in the building of this bridge for your village? Together we can change our fate and bring a blessing to our lives and our families."

The thief smiled at his new friend. "I am honored to have a noble *Viên Quan* help in the building of this bridge. Together we will create a blessing. Together we will build a strong bridge as a testimony to our families' honor.

"People in the region will use this bridge for good purposes. They will cross the river in safety and transport goods for the benefit of all the people. I am sure the Buddha will see and witness our good intentions so that we will both share His blessings."

The two continued to talk, shared more stories about their families, and decided to join together as brothers. The *Viên Quan* would be the older brother and the thief the younger brother. The younger brother shared about his mother, how she was poor and old, working day and night to sell twigs of wood and keep the house together.

"Don't worry," said the *Viên Quan*. "She is now my mother and I come from a wealthy family. I shall take good care of *our* mother. Do not worry anymore, younger brother. Now we can both devote our time to the building of the bridge."

Both were happy, and they embraced to celebrate their new friendship and brotherhood.

Together, the two brothers began working on the wooden bridge, each day going into the forest to select the necessary trees for the support, and cutting the wood to the exact shape necessary to build the broad pathway over the river. Within six months, working day and night with the help of the village people, the bridge was completed!

People came from near and far to see the bridge. They were excited to know they could cross the river in safety and sell their merchandise in the nearby city. They named the new structure "The Blessing Bridge."

All the elders came together to make the proclamation that there would be a celebration feast, collecting money from all the people to buy the best food and drink so they could toast younger brother and older brother they all saw as heroes. Many generations from the villages around would be able to use this bridge for selling their produce. It was seen to be an economic miracle!

On the celebration day, all the people came together, singing, dancing, and eating from the great feast that was prepared. Even Master Teacher was in attendance with his students. They all offered a thanksgiving to the Buddha, then selectively danced a jig of joy for the Blessing Bridge. None of the elders could remember when there had been a happier day in the history of the village.

Then, a strange occurrence took place. Just after midnight, when the people were still dancing, eating, and enjoying themselves, a sudden wind developed, like a twister, and the trees and the earth began to shake.

In seconds, the twister descended upon the younger brother and carried him away into the sky. The *Viên Quan* ran to catch him and pull him to the ground, but it was too late. The twister had carried him high above the trees, and he disappeared into the sky.

The *Viên Quan* called out for him through the night, searching in the forest for his younger brother, but he could not be found. All the people from the village were in shock.

For days, the people in the village were in mourning. Master Teacher led prayers for the people, incense was burned before the Buddha day and night, but younger brother did not return.

The *Viên Quan* cried aloud and could not be comforted. His mother wore the dark clothes of mourning and poured ashes on her head morning and night. She decided to live with the *Viên Quan*, but her tears were for the son who had the vision to build the Blessing Bridge.

The twister had taken the younger brother to the highest mountain beyond the village and above the clouds. He found himself before a cave.

Miraculously, the twister transformed itself into an elder with a long, white beard and flowing, purple robe. He was a majestic figure. Then he spoke. "I am the Wind Spirit. Do not be afraid. I have been sent from God. He has seen all the wonderful things you have done and how you have changed your ways from being a thief to becoming a hero for your village. You have wiped clean your family stain. Dignity and nobility have descended upon your family name. Your honesty, hard work, and kindness will be rewarded.

"Go into the Cave of Treasures. God has given you permission to take all the gold, silver, and precious pearls you can carry. Take as much as you want. We know you will use these treasures for good. You will share this fortune with those who are in need. Go and enjoy your reward."

Younger brother looked into the cave and could not believe his eyes. The gold, silver, and precious pearls were sparkling in the darkness of the cave. Some pieces were the size of a door. Others the length of a man's arm. There were diamonds and rubies the size of chicken eggs.

Younger brother fell on his knees, thanking God and praising the Buddha. He could not believe his good fortune. His desire to live the good life had brought him and his family a blessing. He cried a happy tear, then gathered all the gold, silver, and precious stones he needed into a large sack provided by Wind Spirit. He only gathered what he knew he could carry. Then, Wind Spirit transformed himself into the twister and carried him back to his village, back to the home of his older brother and mother.

His mother and brother could not believe their eyes. They jumped for joy. They had thought him dead, but now he was alive. Not only was he alive, but he had returned with a fortune.

That same evening, they created an altar in their home, lit incense, and together as a family said prayers of thanksgiving.

And the blessings continued. That same year, the *Viên Quan* and his wife had a child. Also, younger brother got married and they had a child. Mother had become a grandmother twice over! In time, the children would go to school with Master Teacher.

All these things took place in the village that was home to the Blessing Bridge.

Born Again as a Hen
Kiếp Sau là Con Gà Mái

*O*nce there lived a young girl, born into a wealthy family, and because she was an only child, she was extremely spoiled. Her name was Thike. Thike was given all manner of things by her family and did not care to know the value of anything.

When lunch or dinner was served, always with rice, she would only take a little rice and throw the rest away. She threw the rice into the trash, sometimes into the flowerbeds, often into the garden path in the back yard. The hens that lived in the back garden really appreciated the rice on the path as they pecked their gentle way to happiness.

Suddenly, Thike became seriously ill and died.

Her soul was sent to the Emerald Courtroom and she was placed before an ancient judge. He was severe looking in his countenance.

"Stand still, young lady, and listen carefully to what the prosecutor has to say about you."

The prosecutor stood up. He was such a small man that when he stood up, he did not seem any taller than when he was sitting. Also, he was thin and had a large, sharp nose. Prosecutors always tend to have large, sharp noses. Nobody really knows why, but they tend to come in handy to accommodate the wire-rimmed spectacles that always hang from the tip.

"What is your name?" the prosecutor asked.

"Thike," she replied in a nervous voice.

"How old are you?" he continued.

"Seventeen," she replied. Actually she was sixteen and a half, but even in the Emerald Courtroom she wanted to impress.

"Do you know why you are here?"

"Certainly not. I am sure it is a mistake. I come from a wealthy family, and I have never done anything wrong. Well, that is not exactly true. Once I stole a cooked egg from my father's plate when he was not looking, but I did not like the taste. Too salty. So I put it back."

Although she was nervous, Thike could still be haughty. Of course, she did not know it.

She behaved in the courtroom as she behaved in life. The prosecutor felt the proceedings were getting away from him.

"Listen here young lady, you are here because you do not know the value of things. Life is really all about things. If you disrespect the things that make up life, you disrespect life itself."

"What do you mean?" she protested.

"Well, let me give you an example. Rice."

"What?"

"Rice. You disrespected rice, Thike. Rice for our people is life. You, when you were living, never for one minute considered the value of rice. You never thought about how much work is endured by the laborers in the rice paddies, not to mention the contribution from Mother Nature (*Thiên Nhiên*). All combine to the nurturing and growing of rice. You did not appreciate this fact. Indeed, you disrespected all the hard work that goes into the growing of rice before it gets into your bowl at the table."

"How did I disrespect it?" Thike could be very feisty!

"Do not argue with me." The prosecutor was getting angry; indeed, at one point, his spectacles fell off his nose and landed on the solid wooden desk where he kept his notes.

The judge interrupted. Although he was severe looking, he was known to have a gentle spirit. "Thike, you are not here because somebody made a mistake. God would not permit you being brought here if you did not deserve it. Rice is not simply rice. Rice is the land. Your country. The foundation on which you live; not just you–all the people. Rice is the soil, the water. It involves the climate, the temperature, the sun and moon. It needs to be planted at the right time in the right way. There is a natural order to the growth of the seed.

"After it is planted, it needs to be respected and loved because rice is life. There is a cycle involved in the replanting of the seed. At the right time. In the right way. Under the right conditions."

The severe looking judge, who had a gentle spirit, always had a way with words.

"Oh Thike. You see white rice in a bowl, but if you only had the spiritual eyes to see, you would experience in that bowl of rice the true nature of existence, civilization, and yes, real religion. How can you respect God if you do not respect what God has created? You, young lady, are not just a pretty girl. You came from a process. So does the rice. The field needs to be plowed, fertilized, and smoothed before the rice is planted. The plants need to grow and mature. The rice needs to be harvested, threshed, and separated from the chaff."

"But—" She tried to interrupt.

"Shh! Then it is washed, rinsed, and finally, do you hear me, finally, cooked and placed in your little bowl. Rice, Miss Thike, is the parable of creation."

"Wow," said Thike. "I am sorry, Mr. Judge. I am sorry, Mr. Prosecutor."

"Be quiet." Now the prosecutor got a chance to speak. He was always a little hesitant before this impressive judge. He nervously played with his spectacles, which made him appear slightly humorous. "Oh yes, we know your family is wealthy and you could say why worry about a little rice? We can afford to throw away rice. But you cannot afford to throw away life. And as you heard the revered judge say, rice is life."

The prosecutor looked slyly in the direction of the judge. Although they were in the Emerald Courtroom, he was not beyond trying to impress!

He continued, "So you see, Miss Thike, this is a most serious case. Some have been known to compare the waste of rice with murder. Remember, to waste is to kill."

Thike gasped. She felt a vapor coming on. She reached for a sip of water.

"Oh yes, to waste rice is a most serious offense," the prosecutor continued. "You are insulting creation. You are insulting the creator. A blasphemy before God."

Thike began to cry.

"I am asking the judge to condemn you to Level Nine in the Chamber of Atonement. You should remain there, existing, until you have learned your lesson."

Thike cried aloud. With tears running down her face, she begged not to be sent to Level Nine in the Chamber of Atonement. Anything but that!

However, it must be stated for the record that Thike had really no idea what Level Nine in the Chamber of Atonement was, but it sounded awful!

The judge again spoke, "Miss Thike, I understand your tears. Sometimes we have something in life to cry about. You must learn from what you have heard. However, nobody can run from the waste and destruction they create. Life has consequences. You cannot run from the negative attitudes and destructive behaviors you have lived. However, I will listen to your plea on your own behalf before I pronounce your sentence."

"Your Honor, I am more than grateful you have given me time to plead on my own behalf. After listening to you and Mr. Prosecutor, I realize I am guilty of disrespecting rice. I had no idea about the spiritual dimension you have explained concerning the waste of food, especially rice. I am not a bad person. I have been an ignorant person. But I have never killed anyone. I have never robbed anyone, except that salty egg from my father that I replaced after tasting it. I have never abused anyone. And so, I think it is unfair for me to be sent to Level Nine in the Chamber of Atonement.

"I do not want to blow my own trumpet, but this is surely the time for me to remind you and Mr. Prosecutor of the good things I did in my life. I remember how I would bring money and food, yes, often it was the rice I did not eat at my table, to the poor and homeless. But I did try to help them. There were more than 20 times I burned incense in the temple before Lord Buddha, and lit a candle for my family. I remember I saved some people from tragic accidents, occasionally risking my own life and–" Thike broke down crying. It is hard to hear your life, especially the destructive behaviors, revealed in a Heavenly Court.

"Now, now, Miss Thike, settle down." The judge seemed genuinely concerned. "Somebody bring her some water, maybe a glass of goat's milk and some sweet rice."

Then, the judge directed his gaze toward the prosecutor. "Mr. Prosecutor, will you check the Calendar of All Good Deeds and see if what Miss Thike is saying is indeed recorded?"

A gentle creature, not unlike the mighty hawk that flies in the forest, appeared at the side of Thike. It had beautiful wings and a most loving countenance, wearing a small green hat and delightful yellow flower. The creature was holding in its claws a cup of goat's milk and a small bowl of sweet rice.

Soon the courtroom was filled with the aroma of sweet rice. The Emerald Courtroom certainly was a most unusual place.

The prosecutor busied himself looking through the pages of a large red book with gilt-edged pages. The book was bigger than he was!

"It is all true, your Honor. It says clearly that Miss Thike did indeed feed the homeless and give them money; on 23 occasions she visited the Sleeping Buddha Temple and burned incense, and lit candles for her family. On several occasions, she helped people from tragic accidents. On one occasion, she rescued a field mouse from a hungry cat."

The judge nodded in the direction of the prosecutor. Although he still looked severe, his gentle spirit was beginning to show. He turned and looked directly at Thike. She knew he was ready to pronounce judgment. "Miss Thike, please stand. Put your milk down, and wipe the sweet rice from your face. Thank you.

"I appreciate all the good deeds you have done in your life, especially visiting the Sleeping Buddha Temple. Many years ago, I was involved in the building of that beautiful place. A place of peace, harmony, and tranquility.

"However, the good deeds cannot erase the wasteful behavior. For sixteen and a half years, yes, Miss Thike I know you are not yet 17, I see you have led a mixed life, not all bad, but certainly not all good. It is the waste of the rice that most concerns me. Wasted food is never good. Often, it creates smelly areas in the garden and those smells can travel into houses through the window and create sickness. Thank God, we have living creatures hidden in the earth that eat up the waste.

Otherwise, people on Earth would surely die from a thousand sicknesses.

"Now, Miss Thike, you really deserve being sent to Level Nine in the Chamber of Atonement. However, I am mindful that you have done good deeds so I want to teach you a lesson–a lesson that could lead to your rebirth.

"I shall send you back to Earth as a hen. You shall return to the family home and spend two years looking for and pecking at spilled rice you find on the garden path and wastelands. Believe me, there is no waste in the life of a hen. Everything is eaten up, even the occasional worm and beetle. More than anything, as a hen, I want you to learn the value of rice and the horror of waste.

"After two years, we shall all meet again, and I will determine how you have behaved, what you have learned, and what shall be your fate for the next life. Now, finish your milk and sweet rice and prepare to live the life of a hen!"

So each time we pass a farm and see all the hens running around looking for spilled rice, grain, or corn on the ground, we should remember the story of Thike. Like her, they may be people who are searching desperately to correct their wasted lives with the hope and dream of a better life when they come to be judged in the Emerald Courtroom.

The Monk and His Disciple
Sư Thầy và Học chò Tu

Hundreds of years ago, there was a most revered monk who had committed himself to the Buddha's teachings for over 30 years. His discipline was admired throughout the land and many disciples in training sat at his feet, listening to every word. Indeed, some disciples felt spiritually transformed just kneeling in his presence.

This monk lived in an ancient temple high in the mountains, because it was believed a holy place needed to be built close to the heavens. Ordinary people from the surrounding villages, as well as monks in training, climbed up this mountain for worship and sacred counsel.

Though there were peacocks and monkeys in the gardens, an atmosphere of holy silence emanated from the temple. It was a special place.

Living at the temple was a very devout disciple called Tu. He was in his twenties, but his learning and discipline made him wise beyond his years.

Tu had great respect for the revered monk and often sought him out for counsel and confession. He had been in training for over ten years, but his intention was to live his life at the temple.

One day, the revered monk and Tu were practicing *khất thực* (begging for food) while taking a trip to a village in the eastern region. They needed to cross a wide river, but it was the summer season, and much of the river had dried up into a sticky, cloying mud.

Monk blessed the mud, saying to Tu that even the mud had a place in God's creation. Indeed, Monk picked up some mud and smelled it as if it had the aroma of a gardenia.

"God is so wonderful and diverse. See the lotus flowers near the bank, swaying their gentle bodies and smiling at the sun? They thrive in the texture of the mud. Thank you, Brother Mud, for the generous feeding of the lotus flowers."

"Come Tu, we need to walk through Brother Mud to the boat waiting for us in the flowing river."

Tu led Monk through the mud in the direction of the boat. As they negotiated their steps, Monk turned and saw two beautiful young women downstream, also trying to cross the mud to their boat.

They looked exquisite in their silk dresses and decorative pearls, but at the same time, they were fearful as they jumped from one steppingstone to the other alongside the muddy bank. Monk looked at them with a gentle smile, admiring their beauty and gentleness. Monk recognized God's beauty in everything.

Tu turned and saw Monk admiring the beautiful women. He observed the smile on Monk's face and the rapt attention he was giving them.

Also, he noticed the young women were looking intently at Monk. Tu was disturbed. Indeed, he felt anger percolating through him, directed toward Monk.

Tu knew the two young women. It was Miss *Ngọc* and her personal servant. *Ngọc* always looked beautiful in his eyes, although he tried not to look when they passed each other in the local market.

He also felt attracted to the servant girl, but pushed such thoughts out of his mind. He refused to admit such feelings even to himself.

Then, Monk walked in the direction of the two young women. He gently kowtowed to them both. They returned his respectful gestures, then Monk said, "Let me assist you. Brother Mud is dirtying your shoes and silks, but he means no harm."

He then took their hands and helped them into their boat. Tu observed Monk as he lifted each woman into the boat, gently smiling at their faces. Tu could not believe his eyes.

Then, Monk pushed their boat in the direction of the bank, waving goodbye as he did. Tu witnessed Monk watching the women negotiate the river for many minutes as they gently waved goodbye to him.

Smiling with deep spiritual contentment, Monk returned to Tu. They continued their mission, practicing *khất thực* in the village.

Nothing was said about the two women, and Tu kept his resentment and judgments to himself. After seven days, they returned to the temple.

That evening, after prayers and meditation before the Great Buddha statue in Jasmine Hall, Tu retired to his cell. But he could not sleep. He tossed and turned all night, consumed with the vision of Monk lifting *Ngọc* and her personal assistant into their boat and smiling at their faces.

"How could the master touch them? He knows it is forbidden for a monk in the service of the Buddha to have close contact with any female.

"And that smile–it was a smile of passion. My master has betrayed his calling. He has given himself over to the sin of impurity. Maybe the two women put a spell upon him, tempted him away from the Rules of Discipline, and ruined him as a master monk. He even gazed at them long after he had returned them to their boat. He enjoyed touching their bodies. He enjoyed their beauty."

Tu felt everything Monk had taught him was null and void. Monk had revealed his hypocrisy and weakness at the river, but it had also affected Tu. He felt he could no longer be a disciple at the temple.

Tu would abandon his training. He would leave his home at the temple immediately.

Early the next morning, with anger and sorrow in his heart, Tu went to see the revered monk. In his cell, as Monk was saying his gratitude prayers, Tu confronted him.

"Holy Master, Vessel of the Divine Spirit, I come to you with sadness and yes, I must admit, anger in my heart. I wish to leave the temple. I can no longer be your disciple."

"Why is this happening, my son? What has transpired to turn you away from your sacred discipleship?"

Tu was nervous and hesitant, but he knew he needed to speak what was in his heart. "It is because of what you did, Holy Master, at the river with the two women, *Ngọc* and her personal assistant."

"Ah, you know them, Tu?"

"Well, yes, I mean, not really. I have seen them. But I did not look at them. I mean they passed me in the market."

"Yes, I understand. Please continue," said Monk.

"I saw you smile at the two women. I could tell you were admiring them. You touched them and helped them into their boat. You continued to smile and wave at them and were, for a time, consumed by them."

Tu could feel the anger rising in his voice as he knelt before Monk. "You were enjoying their beauty. It was a man-woman thing. You ceased to be, for me, a monk. You were a man. A man with feelings.

"You showed me the dark side of life, and I hate you for it." As Tu knelt before Monk, he began to cry. Then, he began to beat his arms against the stone floor.

"I hate you for showing me such feeling. You failed as a monk. I cannot respect you for this. I must leave immediately."

A grave silence fell upon them both. Then Monk spoke hesitantly, "My dearest son, Tu, you are a good disciple, devout and disciplined, and meticulous about your sacrifices. But you have much to learn before you can truly follow the heart of the Buddha. Tu, the heart is not the same as the Rules of Discipline.

"Before you can become a monk, you must first become a man–a man who knows his feelings, so he can live with them, harmonize with them, and love them–not conquer them! Lord Buddha has sent you a great lesson. I did not know it was happening, but I am grateful. It is the crossroad in your discipleship.

"Let me speak to your complaint against me. Yes, I gazed upon the two women, and I admired their beauty. They also are creatures of God. I bless the mud. I bless the lotus flower the Great Buddha rests upon. I welcome Brother Sun, Moon, and Rain. Why not women?"

"But we are told in the Rules of Discipline to avoid the attraction of women," murmured Tu.

"That is true. But first we must understand what the rule is saying. A spiritual rule is never 'against' something; rather, it is always 'for' something. You must digest this wisdom.

"A monk's life is not that of a regular man. We bless family–husband, wife, and children. But that life is not for Monk. And we chose not to give energy to a sexual passion–even if we feel it."

"How can we feel it?" asked Tu.

"How can we not? We are men. God calls men to be monks, not eunuchs. That is a special category. A monk who does not feel cannot live the Rules of Discipline given by the Buddha. I have feelings, Tu, but I transform them to a love for life. All life.

"I smile at the sun. I smile at the insects. Of course, I will smile at women when it is appropriate.

"And at the river, it was appropriate. They were stuck in the mud. Their clothes were wet and soiled. They needed help to get into their boat. I helped them. And I smiled, and waved. And you know, Tu, I still remember that wave and that smile. And it is a good feeling. To help is a good feeling."

Tu cried aloud, "I hate feelings! They make you feel!"

"I know. I know. But to feel is to love. A life without love is an empty life. Maybe this is not about me. It seems as though it is, but maybe it is about you–Tu the man, not the disciple.

"The feelings you ascribe to me, maybe they are yours–yours to deal with. The passion. The sexual energy. The desire. The craving. They were never mine, but maybe they are yours. A true monk must be an honest man and face his feelings, not to conquer them, but to love them– embrace them and harmonize with them."

Tu listened as Monk continued.

"Tu, I carried those two women into the boat seven days ago. You are still carrying them now. Let go. Let go of them and embrace the lessons you must learn in your life." Monk smiled at Tu and helped him to his feet.

"Already you are looking taller."

"Thank you, Master"

Tu was embarrassed and a little confused. "Master, I am very confused. Shall I stay or shall I go? What should I do?"

"First, it is good to be confused. Second, when you are not sure what to do, better not do anything. The gong is sounding. Breakfast awaits. Tomorrow is another day."

Tiger and Little Toad
Hổ và Cóc Con

One summer morning, Little Toad was moving slowly among the sweet potatoes. It was before sunrise, and a thick mist had descended on the ground. Little Toad did not mind the mist because it left drops of sweet dew on the leaves that served as a refreshing drink as he searched for his early breakfast. Little Toad loved breakfast, but he also enjoyed lunch and dinner. Truth be told, Little Toad loved eating!

As he looked intently for some scrumptious leaf insects that were also just waking up, Little Toad was confronted by Big Tiger, who angrily stared down at him.

"What are you doing in my path, you ugly, dirty toad? How dare you hop in my way? Move over quickly or I'll squash you into the ground."

Little Toad was scared and moved quickly; actually, it was slowly compared to most other creatures, because we must remember he was a toad and could only hop an inch or two at a time! But eventually, he was able to hop to the side and let Big Tiger pass.

The sweet potato field had been the home of Little Toad for years until Big Tiger decided to move into the neighborhood. Big Tiger was a bully and always enjoyed picking on Little Toad. He made fun of his little legs, warty skin, and bulging eyes.

At times, he called him "Wart Food" and occasionally picked him up in his huge teeth and threw him in all directions. The other creatures in the area laughed when they saw Big Tiger shaming Little Toad, but secretly, they felt sorry for him, and when Big Tiger had left, they comforted him.

Skinny Rat used to say to Little Toad, "One day, your time will come. You will shame that arrogant tiger at his own game. God will show you a way."

But Little Toad felt sad. He did not know why Big Tiger enjoyed bullying him. He never intended to annoy him.

Often, he hid among the sweet potatoes for days to avoid meeting Big Tiger. He prayed that Skinny Rat's words would come true. "You will shame that arrogant tiger at his own game."

The day came when Big Tiger was feeling bored and decided he would search out Little Toad for some bullying games. "Wart Food, where are you? Come out and face me, you ugly toad. Where are you web-feet?"

"I'm over here Big Tiger." Little Toad had just finished breakfast and was preparing for lunch. He was enjoying a drink near the stream where the leaf insects loved to play.

Big Tiger roared and took two huge strides to tower over Little Toad. "I thought I told you to keep out of my way. Why are you always hopping around in my territory? Wherever I am, you seem to be feeding your ugly little body. Do you enjoy annoying me?"

"Nothing could be further from the truth, Big Tiger. I spend my day trying to avoid you. I hate seeing you–I mean I hate irritating you."

"So, Wart Food doesn't like me? You try to avoid me do you? That's not very nice. Your existence is dependent upon me, you ungrateful creature."

"Please do not roar, Big Tiger. It hurts my head. Do not get angry. I'm only Little Toad. I'm far too small to irritate you."

Big Tiger was getting angrier. His tail was swishing in all directions.

At one point, it hit Skinny Rat across the face, but Big Tiger was so preoccupied with roaring at Little Toad, he did not feel anything.

"But you do irritate me, Wart Food. Just seeing you irritates me. Often I ask myself, 'How can an ugly creature like you live in our neighborhood?' I've decided you should hop out. Move away. Find some other place in the forest to live. I do not want you around anymore."

Little Toad was really agitated. He loved his home among the sweet potatoes, his conversations with Skinny Rat, and his daily diet of leaf insects and sweet dew water.

"But it's been my home for years!"

Big Tiger was unconcerned. He put his huge face in front of Little Toad, so close that Little Toad began to cough at the heated steam coming out of Big Tiger's nostrils. "Hop it, Wart Food. If you're not gone in the hour, I'll crunch your bones into toad paste. Trust me. I can do it."

Little Toad knew he had little time to change the mind of Big Tiger, but he did not want to leave his home, his friends, or his neighborhood. Immediately, he started to think.

"Think, think, think." What could he do? What would help change Big Tiger's mind? He sensed this was the one day Skinny Rat had spoken about "One day your time will come. You will shame that arrogant tiger at his own game. God will show you a way."

But what to do? How to survive? Then it came to him. A challenge. A game. A wager of wits that could fool Big Tiger.

He knew Big Tiger was strong, but he was not very smart. Little Toad trusted his instincts.

"Big Tiger, I challenge you to a game. A competition. A wager between you and me. The neighborhood can be the judges."

"What wager? Are you crazy?"

"If I lose, then you can willingly crush my bones into toad paste, wart food."

"What is the wager, you ugly frog?"

Now Little Toad was angry. Big Tiger had called him many things, but never a frog. The time had definitely come to see who would survive. Little Toad's honor had been insulted.

"I'm a toad. Born a toad. Lived as a toad. Will die a toad. I'm no frog."

"Okay, okay. What is the wager?"

"You see this stream? Well, the wager is to see who can jump the farthest over this stream. If I am able to jump farther than you, then I have won."

"You must be crazy, Little Frog. Not only are you ugly and dirty, you are stupid."

"Let us see," said Little Toad calmly.

When Skinny Rat heard the wager, he was concerned. How could a toad compete in a jump over a stream with a tiger? But he trusted his friend. He knew he was smart.

Nevertheless, he said a quick prayer to the Buddha. "Please, Great Lord Buddha, be with Little Toad in this competition. May he move swiftly to accomplish his task. Amen." Then, Skinny Rat crawled up on a huge stone to observe the proceedings.

Big Tiger could hardly contain his excitement. He moved to the side of Little Toad and kept his eyes looking straight ahead, determining the place where he would land.

"On three," proclaimed Little Toad. "One. Two. THREE!"

As Big Tiger took a deep breath and braced himself for the jump, Little Toad secretly took a gentle bite into the fur of Big Tiger's tail, and when Big Tiger jumped, his tail flipped Little Toad many feet farther along. Big Tiger landed and, with a big smile on his face, proclaimed, "Excellent. I've landed 20 feet beyond the stream. Now, where is that crazy toad?"

"Here I am. I'm back here. Thirty feet beyond the stream. See, I'm back here."

When Big Tiger turned around, sure enough, there was Little Toad. He had outdistanced the tiger.

"I'm the winner!"

Big Tiger was angry and very ashamed. How could Little Toad have jumped farther than he? Maybe he has special powers. Maybe toads have hidden strength. He began to slyly show a little respect for Little Toad, but he was still determined to beat him in competition–and then eat him up.

"Little Toad, may I suggest we play one final game? If you win, I will let you stay in the neighborhood, but if you lose . . ."

"What is the wager?" asked Little Toad. He was feeling confident, and he knew God was with him, even in the trickery. Skinny Rat clapped his paws together in the direction of Little Toad; he knew his prayer to the Buddha had been answered.

"See that oak tree in the far distance? I challenge you to hop to that oak tree before I get there myself. The first to arrive at the oak tree is the winner."

Little Toad thought for a moment. His mind was working fast. But he felt confident God was with him, and he began to develop a plan.

"Okay, okay Big Tiger. The first to arrive at the oak tree. But remember, I have already beaten you once. And I am becoming angry at your bullying and unkind comments.

"Do not annoy me anymore. Do not keep me waiting at the oak tree!"

Big Tiger was surprised at Little Toad's confidence, but he knew he could beat him in a race. How could a hopping toad outrun an athletic tiger? Indeed, he would take his time, give Little Toad a starting chance, take a nap for a few minutes, then run to the oak tree. The neighborhood would see his power and speed, eventually forgetting the wager at the stream, and then, he would crunch up Little Toad.

So Big Tiger told Little Toad to hop along and he took a nap under the tree. Little Toad began to hop toward the oak tree, but he could only move a few inches at a time and he was getting tired. But he had a plan.

He climbed a leafy bush on the path to the oak tree. It was a place he knew well because the leaf insects often made their home in the tree, so he ate a little supper as he waited for Big Tiger to pass by.

Big Tiger eventually woke from his nap under the tree and peered into the distance to see if he could catch a glimpse of the hopping toad. But he could not see anything.

He was not too worried, but he was surprised he could not spot a tired looking toad in the distance. Maybe he needed to move fast, faster than he expected. He began to race toward the oak tree. As he passed the leafy bush, Little Toad jumped onto Big Tiger's back and held on tightly for the duration of the journey. Big Tiger was becoming more anxious and preoccupied as he rushed along the path–not seeing anything of Little Toad–that he never felt the toad clinging to his fur.

Puffing and panting, Big Tiger eventually arrived near the oak tree. Only a few more feet to go. He decided to take a rest. He must have passed Little Toad on the journey.

In his mind, he believed he had already won. Smugly, arrogantly, he decided to take a rest.

This was Little Toad's moment. As Big Tiger rested, he jumped off his back and quickly hopped to the oak tree. He also made sure he had some tiger fur in his mouth. Everything was working out perfectly, and he knew God was with him.

"Where are you? Hey, Stripey stripe. Where are you?" bellowed Little Toad.

"Who's calling?" replied the sleepy tiger.

"It's me. Who do you think? Little Toad. Where have you been? I have been here waiting for hours. And look, see I have had such anger toward you for keeping me waiting that I found a local tiger and ate him up. I've just finished supper. See the fur in my mouth? Remains of your relative! But I am still hungry and angry. I know you are a bully and like most bullies, I believe you are a coward. So guess what? I'm coming over there, and I'm going to eat you up. You see, I'm small but powerful. My God is with me."

When Big Tiger heard this he was amazed and afraid. He had lost both competitions. After each wager, Little Toad had grown stronger and more confident. He did not want to challenge him again.

"Do not come over here, Little Toad. I am going away. I will never trouble you again. I am leaving the neighborhood. You can have it. Goodbye."

And Big Tiger left, never to return again. Little Toad returned to his sweet potato home, ate sumptuously every day on the leaf insects, and enjoyed life.

Skinny Rat never asked Little Toad how he had made Big Tiger leave, but he knew, somehow, his prayer to the Buddha had been answered.

Hunter
Tràng Đi Săn

L ong ago, an experienced hunter lived in a distant land. He surely had a name, but nobody ever used it; people called him Hunter.

Every day he went out hunting, sometimes in the morning, sometimes in the afternoon, but never in the evening. All experienced hunters know it is not smart to hunt in the dark.

The monks, who, as you know, pray every day, teach the people that God sends the darkness so we can rest. Hunter always listened to the wisdom of the monks.

Hunter only killed what he needed for the day. Nobody ever accused him of being a greedy hunter. Always, he returned with something: a deer, goat, wild boar, or at the very least, a skinny rabbit.

At that time, a cruel King ruled the kingdom. Everybody agreed he had ruled for far too many years. He seemed to derive pleasure from being angry, vindictive, and selfish.

Eating meat was his passion, and he always demanded fresh meat, preferably still on the bone. Breakfast, lunch, dinner, and yes, even supper, you would see the King eating his meat and crunching the bones.

The officials at the court, together with the King's generals and captains of the armies, truly feared the cruel King. As such, they tried to please his every whim, developing an equally unhealthy obsession for fresh meat, cooked on the bone.

Occasionally, an inexperienced servant would place vegetables, fruit, and nuts on the table only to be screamed at by the

King. "Do I look like a rabbit? Are you trying to poison me with fruit and nuts? Bring me meat and wine immediately or I'll have you cooked to the bone in the oven!"

The diet the King and his officials lived on was dull and unhealthy, but nobody expressed a word of criticism. In those days, kings could be unhealthy and nobody was allowed to say anything.

One day, the King woke up in a worse mood than usual. He had eaten too many chicken bones the night before, and his stomach ached *(dau bụng)*; even the servants in the far away kitchen could hear his stomach rumble. This usually preceded an oncoming temper tantrum that was about to burst.

Sure enough, the King called together his generals and captains of the armies and sent out a decree to all the four corners of his kingdom: "Every male over the age of 14 must hunt down a wild animal and bring it to the King. The animals must be caught that day and delivered to the castle before sunset.

"Those who catch nothing will be locked in a dark and dirty dungeon for one week as punishment."

Kings at this time often issued inhumane, crazy, and unfair decrees and placed them upon the backs of the people. This King was no exception.

The people could only smile at the King's cruel eccentricities, but behind closed doors, they complained at his unreasonableness. Nevertheless, they had to endure him.

So all the fathers and their sons over the age of 14 ventured out the following day with fear and trepidation, trying to hunt down any wild animals and deliver them to the King before sunset. They hunted from early morning to late afternoon.

They climbed mountains, searched forests, and explored meadows; not a burrow, tree, or stone was left unexamined, yet they caught nothing. It seemed as if somebody had magically whispered the King's decree into the ears of all the wild animals, and they all went into hiding.

No animal cry or shriek of the hawk could be heard in the land. The dis-spirited men returned to the King empty-handed.

"Great, noble, and generous King, we beg for your mercy. We have spent all day hunting in your kingdom and obeying your decree, eager to bring home to you whatever we could catch. But after searching all day, we have found nothing."

The King had been nursing an angry pain as he held his grumbling stomach. He naturally had an unhealthy red-purple complexion, but now, it was even more flushed with rage as he brushed aside the pitiful pleas of his people:

"Shut up. Do not say another begging word. I cannot believe you have failed to hunt down a single animal–not even an emaciated rabbit, sickly mouse, or starving sparrow. You bring nothing for my table. I cannot believe it."

At that moment, a rumbling explosion emanated from the King's stomach. Everybody embarrassingly looked at each other, but nobody said a word.

"You insult your King. And so you will be punished. I shall not only arrest and place in my dark, dirty dungeons all the men and their sons over 14, I shall lock up all your families–wives, mothers, and children. Everybody will be made to suffer."

Another stomach explosion erupted.

Again, nothing was said. The young men wanted to laugh, but fear kept everybody silent. Then Hunter stepped forward.

Hunter had heard the cries of the people. Being cunning as well as wise, the skills required for an excellent hunter, he kneeled before the King, knowing this would make a weak and insecure ruler feel strong, maybe even powerful.

"Your majesty, let the people remain free. I promise on my oath as a hunter that I will bring you the greatest animal in your kingdom. It will provide you with abundant tender meat. Believe me, you, together with your generals, captains of the armies, and court officials, will be able to feast with wine, dance, and merriment."

The King listened intently. He knew Hunter to be a man of his word. He was intrigued as he held his churning stomach, still growling intermittently. His anger subsided as he heard the gentle words Hunter spoke. However, his vindictive nature soon returned as he addressed Hunter:

"Hunter, I accept your pledge to me as an experienced hunter. But be warned, and let everyone present hear my words: if Hunter fails to bring to me, before sunset tomorrow, the greatest animal in my kingdom, then I will chop off his head!"

He looked over and smirked. "Nothing personal, Hunter. The job of a King is not an easy one."

Facing the people once more, the King added, "Then, I will kill one member of each family in my kingdom–each and every day of the year."

An audible gasp burst from the people listening to the King. Even the generals and captains of the armies appeared surprised. Women and children sobbed.

As the King sadistically pronounced his warning, a strange, embarrassing, and offensive odor erupted from the vicinity of his stomach.

Hunter and the people left the presence of the King eagerly. The generals, court officials, and captains of the armies had to remain, meekly smiling as they discreetly covered their noses with their hands or silk handkerchiefs.

Morning came, and it was bitterly cold. Hunter went out with his trusty crossbow and knife, ready to hunt down the greatest animal in the kingdom.

The weather hailed down rain and sleet, yet nothing stopped Hunter from trekking the mountains, searching the forests, and exploring the meadows. However, he could find nothing. It seemed as if every creature had heard the King's decree and gone into hiding.

Exhausted, Hunter did what he had always done when he was angry, tired, and confused; he took out his flute and began to play. The music created a solace that calmed his desperate feelings.

Then he heard a sound. A human voice. A raspy human voice:

"Hey Hunter, why do you come to the forest on such a cold and miserable day? This is not a good day to hunt. Nobody hunts in the rain. The only thing you will catch today is a cold! Come over here and tell me why you are tramping these wet forests."

Hunter walked in the direction of the voice. Soon, he came upon an old lady with silver hair and wrinkled skin; but she had the most delicious smile.

"Even if it snows, I must continue to hunt. The King, who has a very angry stomach and an even uglier temper, has decreed if I do not bring him the greatest animal, he will chop off my head and kill a member of each family for every day of the year.

"He is a very cruel and vindictive King. So now you understand, dear lady, why I am hunting on this cold and miserable day."

The old lady held her chin and nodded her head knowingly. Rasping, she continued, "Oh dear, dear. In exchange for animal meat the King is willing to create such havoc, pain, and misery among his people. Gracious me. What a tragic man he is. The chicken bones and livers he consumes have suffocated his feeling heart. No wonder he has a rotting stomach. He is a crazy man. More, he is a cruel crazy man. No creature–animal or human–is safe in his kingdom. Come with me, Hunter."

Hunter sensed the old lady knew him, but he could not remember ever meeting her. Yet Hunter knew that in life some people know other people through instinct. Animals naturally have this recognition, and Hunter had developed it during the time he had lived in the forest.

Oh yes, the old lady knew him.

As Hunter followed the old lady up the mountain, they arrived at a cave. It had a peaceful atmosphere and the old lady had obviously made it her home. She walked with a delightful shuffle to the far corner of the cave and returned carrying something.

It was a fox. A beautiful, little white fox *(sóc trắng nhỏ)*. It had yellow-brown eyes and a most serene expression. It obviously enjoyed being carried in the old lady's arms.

"I want you to take this fox to the King. Trust me, all the hopes and wishes you and the people desire will be granted. But you must trust me.

"I am going to place this fox in your arms, and please do not put it down or expect it to walk. I do not wish it to become tired. It must be strong for the work it is about to do. Remember, Hunter, things are not always what they seem. We must be able to look beyond appearances."

Hunter looked quizzically at the old lady. At the same time, he instinctively trusted her. Then he began his journey, carefully carrying the little white fox to the castle.

The King was sarcastically amused when Hunter presented the little white fox before the assembled court. He sniggeringly complained that the animal was too small, having little meat.

111

Laughing, he poked the fox. Then, the King's stomach gently rumbled, but it was drowned out by the jeers and laughter from the generals, captains, and court officials.

"You call this the greatest animal in the kingdom?" They sneered.

Then the King looked suspiciously at Hunter. "What are you up to? You surely are not serious? Is this some kind of joke? Whatever it is, you are playing a very dangerous game."

At that very moment, the little white fox uttered a cry and grew three times its normal size. Now it was the size of a wild boar.

The King, generals, captains, and court officials were all amazed at the miraculous growth of the little white fox. Still, they were not satisfied.

"You will have to do better than this, little fox," exclaimed the King.

Again, the white fox uttered a cry, and it again grew three times its normal size. It was now the size of a huge buffalo.

The King and everyone at the court were amazed, including Hunter. For the first time in six years, the King's stomach ceased to rumble and growl. Everyone was mesmerized to see a little white fox the size of a buffalo!

The King, generals, captains, and court officials were very happy and about to jump for joy, thinking about the meat and bones they would soon be enjoying. Then, the white fox moved into the center of the great room.

It roared with the loudest voice anybody ever heard in the kingdom. The sound resonated through the deepest part of the forest, reaching the tops of the highest mountains, echoing along the meadows.

The roar was deafening. All the windows in the castle instantly cracked. Then, an eerie silence fell upon everyone.

Hunter wondered what would happen next. Not a word was spoken.

Then, the white fox turned and looked directly at the King with fiery red eyes. It was the stare of death.

Suddenly, the silence was broken by the noise of a mighty stampede shaking the castle. The sound of galloping hoofs and roaring animals filled the air. Dust started to fall from the ceilings and the castle shook due to an approaching earthquake.

The doors burst open and every species of wild animal that had ever been hunted crashed into the room: lions, tigers, wild boars, bears, goats, antelopes, and angry elephants. All the powerful animals in the kingdom that had ever been beaten, killed, and eaten were now taking their revenge. They had come to hunt down the King and his entourage. The cruel and selfish hunters were now the hunted.

Hunter watched in amazement. The white fox had released nature's powerful forces that seek to bring balance and harmony into every kingdom. It was a time of atonement.

After the cruel King, generals, captains, and court officials were killed, the white fox cried a piercing howl of great beauty. Hunter was familiar with the sound.

It was the music he played on his flute. Within minutes, serenity descended upon the castle.

The white fox returned to its natural size. With stately reverence and natural order, the animals slowly began to leave the castle. The kingdom was at peace.

Soon, all the people from the four corners of the kingdom gathered around the castle, singing, feasting, drinking sweet wine, and dancing for joy. They all instinctively knew harmony and justice had returned to their kingdom. The cruel King was dead.

It was not long before Hunter was elected King. His first decree was to release all the prisoners from the dark and dirty dungeons. Then, he proclaimed that hunting must always be conducted with reverence and respect for every creature.

He suggested it was a good idea to farm chickens, hens, and ducks, enjoying their delicious eggs. He also believed the time had come to work the land, producing vegetables, fruits, and nuts.

A time descended upon this kingdom when the people and the animals lived in harmony together.

Also, a new legend spread throughout the kingdom claiming that occasionally, on a clear night, you can see the Hunter King walking in the forests with a silver-haired old lady and a little white fox.

Golden Hole or Silver Hole

Hố Vàng hay Hố Bạc

Vietnamese Buddhists have a popular saying that goes like this: "If you are too greedy, it will lead to tragedy." Here is a story that illustrates the truth of this moral.

There was once a very rich widower who lived with his two sons. As often happens to rich men who do not have wives, he suddenly died!

Because the death was sudden and unexpected, the rich man had not left a will dividing up his property between his two sons.

The older brother, who all his life had been greedy and selfish, decided to take matters into his own hands. He called his younger brother into the house.

"Dearest brother, the time has come for us to share the possessions our father has left to us. I suggest you take the old house in the northern part of the forest, and I will also give you this beautiful axe *(chiếc riù)* so you can begin building up your new life. I shall stay in this house, the house we grew up in, and keep the money father left for myself so I can continue the business. Remember, I am the older brother and you need to obey my instructions now that father is dead."

The younger brother, truth be told, was rather naïve and trusted the wisdom of his older brother. "Thank you, older brother, for letting me have the house in the northern part of the forest and the beautiful axe with which I can begin working. You really are a generous brother to me, and I appreciate your kindness."

For many months, the younger brother busied himself chopping down trees and building an attractive extension to the house the older brother had given him.

One day, he had worked so hard that he fell into a deep sleep under a huge oak tree that shaded him from the sun. His sleep was so deep and relaxed that night came, bringing a dazzling full moon, and he continued to sleep under the oak tree.

His sleep was so deep and his body so relaxed it was as if he were dead.

Many of the local people called this part of the woods the Magic Forest because stories had been told of wonderful happenings that occurred during the night. Most of these stories involved monkeys.

Although the general public did not know this, there were four gray monkeys assigned to guard the forest and clean up any dead bodies they found in the brush. They carried them to specially designed caves where the dead were rewarded or not for the kind of life they had lived.

You see, Buddhists believe our spirit is rewarded for the kind of life we have lived on Earth.

The four monkeys came across the younger brother in a deep sleep under the oak tree and thought he was dead. They had instincts concerning the soul of each person they encountered and conducted a ritual to determine which of the caves the dead body needed to be carried to. The ritual went like this: two monkeys grabbed the arms, two monkeys grabbed the legs, and they walked around in a circle singing the following chant:

Golden hole or Silver hole
This body has a great soul
But life has been a struggle
Let's take him to the Golden hole

So that very night, the four monkeys carried the younger brother to the Golden hole, which was a special cave buried in the mountain deep within the forest, and covered him with leaves.

The next morning, the younger brother woke from his deep sleep and found himself in the cave covered with leaves. His eyes were dazzled by the glitter of gold that was piled all around him.

He could hardly see or move for the stacks of gold coins that surrounded him. He was overwhelmed with gratitude and immediately said a prayer to the Buddha for such rich blessings.

The younger brother then returned to town the richest man in his region, buying a magnificent house for himself and employing many servants and workers so he could invest his wealth and benefit others.

The older brother eventually heard the news that had befallen his younger brother and went to see him.

"Dearest brother, how did you become so rich so fast? I gave you only the old house in the northern part of the forest and an axe, and you have created a business empire! How did you do it?"

The younger brother answered his older brother honestly, for he was always one to tell the truth.

"Dearest brother, I had been working all day chopping down trees to build an extension on the old house you gave me. I was working in the area the locals call the Magic Forest when I became very tired and took a rest under the shade of a big oak tree.

"My sleep was a deep sleep, so deep that I dreamed I was visited by four gray monkeys who thought I was dead. They lifted me up and performed a ritual on me, singing:

Golden hole or Silver hole
This body has a great soul
But life has been a struggle
Let's take him to the Golden hole

That is all I can remember. The next day, I woke up in a cave surrounded by gold coins. I thanked the Buddha and the rest is how you see it."

The older brother became very excited when he heard the story. The greed that had dominated his life got him thinking about how he could become even richer, becoming the richest man not only in the region, but in the kingdom itself!

So the next night, he embarked on a trek after receiving from his younger brother a map that would take him to the Magic Forest and the exact location of the oak tree. Arriving at the oak tree in the night, he lay beneath it and pretended to be dead.

As the moon rose fully and brilliantly, so emerged the four gray monkeys from the forest. They discovered the body of the older brother lying beneath the oak tree. As usual, two monkeys lifted the arms and two lifted the legs, and they performed their ritual, singing:

Golden hole or Silver hole
This body has no sharing soul
His life has never been a struggle
Let's take him to the Silver hole

The older brother heard the words of the ritual song and became angry because he wanted to be taken to the Golden hole. Silver was good, but he knew real wealth was attained only with gold.

Immediately, his eyes opened up and he shouted, "No! Wait you stupid monkeys! You are taking me to the wrong hole. I want to be taken to the Golden hole. Put me down and show me where I can find the Golden hole."

Now, the four gray monkeys became very frightened because they had never seen a dead body scream and shout before. So they threw the older brother high into the air, almost to the top of the huge oak tree, and they ran away. The older brother landed with a deafening thud, hitting his head against a rock in the forest, and he died immediately.

The four gray monkeys returned the following night and buried the older brother in the ground. They performed no ritual. There would be no reward.

Red Rat with Bulging Eyes
Chuột Lông Đỏ Mắt Lời

Years ago, out in the fields of the Northern territory, two daughters were born to parents who were ordinary farmers. They were not rich, not anything exceptional at all, but a good family.

The daughters were simply named Big Sister (*Cô Cả*) and Little Sister (*Cô Hai*).

Big Sister was very pretty, and she tended to get more affection from her parents. She was manipulative, selfish, and yes, it must be said, a little lazy.

Little Sister tended to be chubby, especially in the cold months when she loved to eat *phở* and rice, but she was always gentle, thoughtful, and very hard working.

125

She loved to help her parents in the fields and regardless of how difficult the jobs were, she never complained; she was always patient.

As the sisters grew into teenagers, they were assigned to the job of taking care of the cornfields. They had a specific responsibility: to remove the unwanted grass and weeds that grew between the emerging young corn.

As the summer season swept the countryside, the young corn grew nicely and the stalks seemed to wave to each other and dance in the soft breeze. Unfortunately, the grass and weeds also grew.

At times, it seemed the weeds were strangling the young corn. So every day, the two sisters came out after their morning bowl of *phở* to perform their job of removing the unwanted grass and weeds.

Big Sister preferred to play with the butterflies and hop along with the speckled field frogs. Little Sister always worked diligently.

She systematically worked the rows of corn, removing the unwanted grass and weeds, working thoroughly and fast. In the patches she worked, only the corn was left standing, beautiful and strong.

But no matter how hard the two sisters worked–and we know Big Sister did not do her share, being distracted by the beautiful butterflies and speckled frogs–the unwanted grass and weeds grew back every few days, especially if it rained. Grass and weeds love to drink rain.

The young corn was growing nicely and would soon be ready for harvesting, but the weeds and grass were also growing, taking away the essential nutrients meant for the corn.

One warm afternoon, after Big Sister had returned from playing near the rippling stream, she wearily took the hand of Little Sister and sighed, "Little Sister, I'm so tired of these objectionable weeds and grass. I really am. Every day we come out to do the same tasks, and every night, the weeds and grass creep back. It is like a sick joke that nature is playing on us.

"I wish, I really wish, there were someone else to do our job, to remove the weeds and grass and keep the corn rows clean and tidy. Then, I would marry that person regardless of how ugly he was."

Little Sister could not believe her ears. "Shh! My Big Sister! You must not say things like that because God is listening. You must not joke in that silly way. Maybe somebody who is really ugly hears you and he comes to remove the weeds and grass, then you would be forced to marry that man.

"Oh dearest sister, you must be careful about what you wish for. You are such a beautiful girl, I cannot bear to think of you marrying an ugly man to honor your promise!"

Big Sister repeated herself in a weary, but determined tone, "I mean what I say. Before the Lord Buddha, I swear that if anyone, and I mean anyone, can come and remove these tiresome weeds and ugly grass, I shall marry him. I know it is hard to believe I would do such a thing, but I will face it should it happen."

Unknown to the two sisters, in a dark hole to the side of them, Red Rat with Bulging Eyes lurked and was listening attentively. He heard all Big Sister said, both her wish and her promise, and he felt happy inside, and a little excited, because he knew he could surely remove all the grass and weeds.

What a great opportunity in his life! He could do what he loved to do, eat the grass and weeds, and in return, he would have a beautiful wife.

Red Rat with Bulging Eyes had been alone for a long time, so he anticipated his future happiness after he had done the job according to Big Sister's wish. Red Rat waited until sunset when the sisters had gone home, and he crawled out of his hole, ready to work.

All night, he waddled up and down the cornrows removing every blade of grass and nasty weed. By sunrise, he had fulfilled Big Sister's wish.

The next morning, the two sisters came to the cornfields, like every other morning, only to find every weed and blade of grass had been removed. The sisters, as far as their eyes could see, gazed only upon healthy rows of corn waving and dancing in the gentle breeze.

The sisters were so happy they danced for joy, imitating the swaying corn. It was a delight to watch.

Little Sister said to Big Sister, " Wow! Look at the corn! Can you believe this miracle? After you made your wish and promise, somebody came out in the night and removed all the grass and weeds. Not a single weed or grass blade remains."

Big Sister was dancing for joy. She was so pleased she did not have to work that day, not that she really worked anyway, finding excuses to go down to the stream to play with the butterflies and speckled frogs.

She was so happy, shouting in a delirious voice, "Oh my God! Thank you Lord Buddha! I cannot stop jumping for joy. Let's call out to see who helped us, who heard my wish, removing all these unwanted weeds and grass, and I will thank him, honoring my promise, face to face. Even if he is ugly, I will marry him."

Red Rat heard Big Sister. He felt very nervous, but he was happy. And he was ready to marry Big Sister.

"Me! It's me! I'm the one who cleaned up all the corn rows. I'm the one who heard your wish and worked all night long to make you happy."

Big Sister could hear the faint voice, but could not see anybody. She never thought to look on the ground. She never thought to look in a rat hole *(lỗ chuột).*

Big Sister called out louder, "Where are you? I hear your gentle voice, but I cannot see you. Speak louder. Come forward. Who are you? Let me see you, my hard working friend who has helped me so much and granted my wish. You are my betrothed!"

Red Rat shouted louder, "It's me. I'm down here. Be very careful where you put your feet or you will stand on me. I'm down here at the entrance to my home."

Big Sister looked all around. First to the left. Then to the right. Then she hesitantly turned her eyes to the ground.

And there he was, waving from his rat hole–Red Rat with Bulging Eyes.

Big Sister could not believe her eyes. She could not believe her ears. A big red rat! She was terrified and started to scream.

Little Sister was still a distance away and had not seen the rat. She called to Big Sister, "What is it? Why are you screaming? What makes you so terrified? Big Sister, please tell me why you are so unhappy and crying."

"Look! Just look at what is waving at me from that hole. Look! It is a big Red Rat with Bulging Eyes! When I made my wish and promise yesterday, I thought it would be a man who would come to help me. A human being!

"Who would believe a big rat with red fur would answer my wish? What can I do now, Little Sister? What can I do?"

Big Sister thought for a minute. She was manipulative. "I know. I shall run away and hide. I will take back my promise. God, Lord Buddha, no living person would expect me to marry a rat!"

Big Sister started to run, running faster than she had ever run before. Remember, Big Sister was quite lazy and rarely ran or worked up a sweat. This time, she ran without looking back.

Red Rat was a little traumatized. He hated noise, especially screaming. But he soon composed himself and decided to run after Big Sister.

Big Sister was a creature of habit, so when she started running, she headed in the direction of the stream. In the shade, a lush fig tree was standing tall. Big Sister quickly climbed the tree to hide from Red Rat with Bulging Eyes.

Red Rat eventually arrived at the stream, but could not see Big Sister, who was hiding in the tallest branch of the fig tree. He began to call out to her in the most endearing and sweet voice, "My dearest, my love, where are you? I know I frightened you, but I really mean you no harm.

"Do not make me chase you like this. Please show yourself. I promise I will not hurt you."

As Big Sister peered down from the branch, she saw her reflection in the clear stream and had an idea. In a gentle, but muffled voice, she cried, "Dear, dear Mr. Rat. I am down here. I am at the bottom of the stream. Look! Can you not see me waving to you? Please dive in and rescue me."

Red Rat waddled over the rocks at the side of the stream and there, looking up at him, he saw Big Sister waving and smiling. He was so excited, happy to find her and pleased she was waving to him.

He immediately dived in to rescue her, but the stream was very deep. With all his strength and his little legs and paws pulling hard, he just could not get to the bottom of the stream.

He tried for many minutes, but he could not do it. Exhausted, he returned to the banks of the stream, fighting to get his breath.

Panting, he cried, "My dearest, my love, I just cannot do it. I am not strong enough to swim to the bottom of the stream. I can see you so clearly, but I cannot reach you."

In between pants and sighs, he muttered, "I am a failure."

Big Sister was very naughty, laughing behind her hand, really enjoying her mean and dangerous game. "Dear, I have an idea. Why don't you find a big rock, like the one you are resting on, and tie it around your neck. Pull it into the stream with you, then you can easily reach the bottom of the stream where I await you."

She uttered the dangerous instructions in the sweetest voice!

Red Rat with Bulging Eyes did exactly what Big Sister asked of him. He was determined to rescue her at any cost.

He found a rope that had been left by the children from the village who always loved to play by the stream, and he tied a big rock around his neck and pulled it in the water.

The rock immediately pulled him to the bottom, but poor Red Rat could not breathe or move. He gasped for air, and as he did, his little stomach filled with water.

He was drowning, but Big Sister did not care. While this was happening, she quickly climbed down the fig tree and ran laughing all the way back to her house.

By this time, Little Sister arrived at the stream. She could not see Big Sister anywhere, but she could see Red Rat with Bulging Eyes struggling at the bottom of the stream with a large rock tied around his neck.

Poor Red Rat! She knew he was drowning and could not let this happen.

Little Sister dived into the water and struggled to pull him and the rock to the side of the stream, because Red Rat had tied the knot tightly to ensure he could reach Big Sister. It was an awesome experience.

Wet and exhausted, Little Sister pulled Red Rat to the bank, removed the rock, and applied gentle pressure to his stomach that was filled with water. She pulled him over to the roots of the fig tree and placed his little head facing the ground, stroking his beautiful red fur while she waited for Red Rat to regain consciousness.

It was at that moment she began to have feelings for Red Rat with Bulging Eyes. What she felt was more than sympathy, more than sadness for the way her sister had treated this loving creature.

Little Sister began to feel affection, real and true affection, for Red Rat. She started to cry, her tears rolling down her cheeks and falling on to the beautiful fur of Red Rat.

As her tears fell, Red Rat started to move and with a big belch, he pushed all the stream water from his stomach. He was slowly coming back to life.

Little Sister was so happy to see Red Rat's eyes open, and soon, they were both looking at each other. Her affection grew. Little Sister and Red Rat had a *connection*.

Then, Red Rat noticed the tear stains on her cheeks and in the gentlest of voices, he asked, "Sweetie, why have you been crying? What has made you so sad?" He looked around. "Where is Big Sister? Is she all right? Please tell me, sweet one."

Little Sister looked at Red Rat with the most loving eyes and said, "I am afraid Big Sister has not behaved well. She not only tricked you at the stream and broke the promise she made to Lord Buddha, but I believe she also tried to harm you. Yet, you were the one who fulfilled her wish.

"I am sorry and so ashamed. Can you forgive her? Can you forgive me, her Little Sister?"

"Sweetie, do not cry anymore. I do not want you to feel sad. It was not you who hurt or tricked me. I can see now that you would never hurt me. Maybe it is too much to expect a beautiful girl to love an ugly rat.

"Thank you for saving my life. I shall be indebted to you forever. It is because of you that I still have a life. Who knows what the future will bring?

"But I have kept you long enough. I have taken too much of your time. Now I should go home. Shall we say goodbye?"

Little Sister did not want to say goodbye to Red Rat. She had real feelings for him; more, much more, than affection.

She did not want to leave him, but she did not want to appear too needy. "Oh my dear Red Rat, it is getting dark and starting to rain. It will take some time for your strength to return fully.

"I do not want you to be alone in your little hole–I mean your home. Please, come with me to my house and let me take care of you. It would make me very happy."

Red Rat was deeply touched. He wanted so much to be with Little Sister, but he dared not request it. He also had a secret he had shared with nobody.

Maybe this noble, gentle, and honest girl was to rescue his life a second time! Only time and love would tell.

"Do you really mean it? Could this be really happening to me? I am such an ugly rat and you, well, you are the gentle and sweet Little Sister.

"Would it really be all right for me to come and live with you? I cannot be your brother-in-law, because your big sister has abandoned me. Well, to tell you honestly, after the way she has behaved, I would not want to be your brother-in-law.

"But if you invite me to stay with you, I promise I will make your life happy and magical. You have saved my life. Now I promise to bring a new life to you."

Little Sister was deeply touched by his words. She sensed something special was happening, but she did not know what. So much had occurred in just a few hours. Now a new adventure awaited her.

Red Rat followed Little Sister to her house. They arrived just before sunset and together they quietly crept into Little Sister's room.

Everybody was sleeping. Nobody knew a mysterious guest had arrived!

The parents of Little Sister and Big Sister always provided abundant food for their children, so it was not too difficult for Little Sister to sneak some rice and chicken or fish for Red Rat with Bulging Eyes, who was hiding in her bedroom. However, it always seemed incredible to Little Sister how much Red Rat could eat!

One bowl, two bowls, sometimes three bowls with extra fruit and vegetables. Whatever Little Sister gave him, Red Rat would eat.

Little Sister knew he was a big rat, but he seemed to eat more than the entire family. Could he be eating for two? Who was he giving the extra food to?

One day, Little Sister pretended to go out to the cornfields with Big Sister, because she continued to work in the fields, never speaking about the horrible incident of the near-drowning of Red Rat. Little Sister made an excuse to return to the house and silently crept to the side window to see what was happening.

She was amazed to see the most handsome man she had ever seen–in her bedroom. He had clear brown eyes; a firm, muscular body; and the most beautiful red hair. He was tidying her room before he ate the bowls of rice and chicken she had prepared for Red Rat.

Intuitively, Little Sister knew the handsome man was Red Rat. She knew that in some strange and miraculous way, Red Rat was able to transform himself into this handsome man.

But how? Why?

This she did not know. And when she saw the handsome man for the first time, she wanted so much to run and hug him, throw her arms around him, and kiss him.

But something inside her told her to wait, and she trusted her intuition. She trusted her instinct to be patient. The last thing she wanted to do was alarm him because she knew this handsome man was her gentle friend Red Rat.

Weeks passed and Little Sister continued to keep the secret. She furtively set aside chicken, fish, vegetables, pork, and rice for Red Rat–really the handsome man.

All this time, Big Sister sensed something. She knew Little Sister was keeping something from her, probably hiding Red Rat in her bedroom, but she could not prove anything.

Occasionally, she would sneak into Little Sister's bedroom in the morning, afternoon, and early evening, but she could never find anything or anyone. If Big Sister could find Red Rat with Bulging Eyes, she would kill him, destroy him, and remove all memory of the promise she had made to God but had not kept. Red Rat could not be found. He had a special hiding place in Little Sister's closet where he felt warm and protected.

Little Sister never said anything to Red Rat about what she had seen through the window, but she showed her love and affection by gently kissing, cuddling, and stroking Red Rat's fur every night and dreaming of the handsome man. In her heart, she knew Red Rat was carrying within him mysterious happenings from long ago. But she was patient. Time, embraced by love, would eventually reveal everything.

One fateful night, Little Sister's mother came into her bedroom. It was something she rarely did, but she was returning a silk scarf that had been left on the kitchen chair.

Mother was exceptionally tidy and hated seeing clothes left around in the wrong place. She was shocked to find Little Sister sitting on her bed, petting the ugly Red Rat with Bulging Eyes.

At first, she could not believe what she was seeing. It was such a strange looking rat. Mother had a rule that all animals and pets stay outside, especially rodents.

Mother was angry at Little Sister and she screamed, "What is that ugly rat doing in this house? How can you pet such an ugly creature? Are you mad? Throw it out immediately or I will kill it with my broom."

Little Sister took a deep breath, said a silent prayer to Lord Buddha, and then exclaimed, "Please, Mother Dearest, I have always been a good, diligent, and hard working daughter, never complaining and happy to obey your rules and instructions all my life. I beg you, please allow me to marry my faithful and loving friend. To you he is an ugly Red Rat with Bulging Eyes, but to me he is a handsome prince. I see beyond the surface, and I know my friend is most special. Please let me marry?"

"Are you crazy?" shouted Mother. "This is a rat. An ugly rat at that. You are a sweet, gentle daughter, obedient and hard working. I thought you would want to marry a man. A handsome man who would take care of you and make you happy as your father has made me happy all these years. You cannot seriously want to marry a rat?"

"Dearest Mother, I am serious. I love my Red Rat. I am happy every moment I am with him. He makes me happy and he truly cares for me.

"Big Sister made him suffer when she broke her promise, but her betrayal became my opportunity. You want me to be happy? Can you not see the happiness we both share?"

Mother's anger surged inside and her face became red. "I know about Big Sister's silly promise. I know she ran away from this ugly Red Rat with Bulging Eyes. I am sorry about that, but I feel the time has come for you to do the same. Take this rat into the cornfields and return him to his hole, then run away. Run away forever. You are a human being and he is a rat. Human beings do not marry rats! It is crazy for you, Little Sister, to think you can live with or marry a rat. People will laugh at you. People will laugh at us. Our good name will be smeared throughout the village. I could not hold my head high in the Temple.

"Now obey my words. Cast away this rat immediately or I will cast you away. I will disown you. It is your family or the rat! If you choose the rat, you must go away, go a long way away. You are not my daughter. That is all I have to say."

Little Sister, with tears rolling down her cheeks, held Red Rat close to her heart, picked up her woolen rug and silk scarf to keep them both warm, and stepped out into the night. She cried for three days,

146

her heart broken at being cast out by her mother, but in her soul she knew she had made the right decision.

Red Rat whispered in her ear, "Everything will be all right. Trust me. One day, this sadness will turn into joy." Then he kissed her with his little lips.

Three years went quickly by. All this time, Mother missed Little Sister. She missed her hard work, cheerful face, and gentle patience. Mother also loved Big Sister, but she knew she was lazy, selfish, and extremely vain. Little Sister, on the other hand, was a gift from God.

One day, Mother decided to go on a journey to find Little Sister. Her anger had tempered, and although she still felt it was crazy for a young woman to love a rat, Little Sister was still her daughter. Blood is thicker than water, and sometimes family affection can overcome dissension.

After weeks of traveling, she eventually found Little Sister in a small farming community. Little Sister was sitting outside her house at a loom, happily weaving and singing. All around her were beautiful fabrics in various colors and near her house, a large field with waving corn. It was a picture of serenity, and Little Sister looked very happy and content.

When Little Sister saw her mother, she ran to embrace her. Past hurts were forgotten. This was her mother. This was family. Mother gently kissed the cheeks of her daughter. It was like old times.

When Mother walked into the house, she found everything neat and tidy. In the backyard were ducks, chickens, and a few small pigs. The house held an air of prosperity.

"Little Sister, you seem very content. I suspect you have a man in you life. A real man, not a rat."

"Now, Mother," murmured Little Sister.

"All right, all right, I do not want to argue with you at our first meeting in three years. I am sure you were very fond of that ugly Red Rat with Bulging Eyes. I know he was fond of you. Why not? You gave him everything."

"Mother!"

"All right, all right, but tell me, Little Sister, when I came into the village, walking through the cornfields close to your house, I saw a most handsome man. He had a proud chin, muscular body, and beautiful red hair. Is he the man in your life?"

"Yes, Mother. He is the handsome man in my life. I love him so much. He works hard, prays morning and night, and is always so gentle with me. However, he is extremely shy. Most times he avoids people. But I am the most fortunate woman in the world."

"Does he allow you to keep the red rat?" Even after three years, Mother could not forget her daughter had eloped with a rat!"

"Mother, he is Red Rat! When he works alone in the fields or is with me at night, he transforms himself into the handsome man you saw in the fields. But I must also be honest with you; there are times, especially when people are around, that he becomes Red Rat. I do not fully understand but because I respect him, I will not speak about it–though it is true."

Mother was amazed. It was incredible the handsome man she saw in the fields could also be Red Rat with Bulging Eyes.

It was like a curse. Hard for the man. Also hard for the rat.

Now, Big Sister had received her cunning and manipulative nature from Mother, who immediately felt the curse needed to be broken, but how? She encouraged Little Sister to think about ways that might prevent the handsome man from transforming into Red Rat.

Slowly, Little Sister began to speak, "Maybe we can destroy the red fur that is in the bedroom. Maybe without the fur, he cannot change!"

"Yes! Yes," shouted Mother. "Show me the fur, Little Sister, and we will put it in the fire. This fur needs to be burned. It cannot be thrown away. It needs to be destroyed."

Immediately after she finished speaking, Mother led Little Sister into the bedroom and soon, they were burning the beautiful red fur.

The moment the red fur was burned, Red Rat, in his human form, felt his skin itch. He instantly knew that something had happened to his fur. He raced back to the house.

Upon entering, he found Mother and Little Sister talking with each other as they drank tea. They were smiling at each other and obviously at peace.

He remembered years ago how angry Mother had been when she had caught Little Sister petting him in his rat form. It was gratifying to see mother and daughter united.

Not one to hold a grudge, he walked over and greeted Mother with a friendly smile. Little Sister introduced them.

"My dearest love, I have something to tell you. Even if what I have done offends you, I hope you will not be too angry with me."

"Is it about the red fur?" he asked.

"Yes, my dear. Mother and I have destroyed it. I know when you are around people, you are often afraid and transform into Red Rat. But I love you and want to marry you. We have lived together happily for more than three years, and now it is time for us to start a family as husband and wife.

"I loved Red Rat, and a part of you will always be the loving creature I met years ago, but I can express my love more fully when you are the handsome man of my dreams, my prince."

The man smiled. There was no anger or fear on his face. He knew what Little Sister was saying was true–more true than she could ever know.

"Dearest Beloved, I am indeed a prince, a prince from the Northern Territory. But I was not a good prince. I was not a good man. It is all in the past now, but I had done some shameful things, and God decided to punish me.

"Overnight, God turned me into the ugly Red Rat and sent me to live in your cornfields. God commanded me to show love, gentleness, and forgiveness; only by living the good life would I find peace and happiness.

"Only when I found the true love of my life could I transform myself back into human form, but I would not be a prince, and I could not stay human permanently.

"When I met you at the stream three years ago, I knew I had found the one I truly loved. And when you committed yourself to me, even as an ugly rat, I knew I could be transformed in your presence. But I was commanded by God not to speak about this curse, and you never asked me about it all these years.

"In your presence, I learned about love. With you, I grew in gentleness. Alongside you, I could forgive."

The handsome man looked intently at Mother. She knew, although he did not speak of it, that he remembered the anguish caused by Big Sister.

She knew he remembered her harsh words when she disowned Little Sister and sent them both out into the cold night, but all Mother saw on the handsome man's face was forgiveness. The true forgiveness that comes from God.

Mother shed a tear of gratitude.

But he had more to say. "Little Sister, your patience has paid off. Your instinct for knowing the time to burn the red fur, even if prompted by your mother, is miraculous. Today is the day God has removed the curse. I have made amends. Genuinely have I embraced the good life, thanks in no small part to your love, patience, and kindness. Tomorrow, I can reclaim my kingdom in the Northern Territory and you will be my Princess."

Little Sister's eyes sparkled with joyous tears. The chickens, ducks, and pigs danced a jig in the backyard. The rows of corn swayed and danced in the wind.

Mother hugged her new son-in-law. And as she did so, she was preparing in her mind the most sumptuous wedding for her loving daughter, Little Sister.

Lazy Man
Thằng Lười

B eyond deep rivers and high mountains, a fig tree *(cây sung)* lived in a beautiful forest. Close to the fig tree was a small village far away from any city, and a small community had lived there for many years.

People in the village worked hard on their farms and vegetable gardens, some even raising their own chickens and pigs. Everyone lived well and enjoyed life.

People from the village often came to admire the fig tree because it was considered magical. It was truly blessed by God. It was tall and healthy and cast the most wonderful shade throughout the year.

Yet the most amazing fact about this fig tree was that throughout the year, it produced the most succulent figs–large, round, and ever so juicy.

There lived, in this village, a very lazy man. Really lazy. He was so lazy he did not even build a home for himself, did no work, cooked no food; indeed, it took him all the effort he could muster just to walk around.

All the other villagers worried because they knew Lord Buddha expected everyone to create their own peace, serenity, and harmony. Nothing ever came from being lazy. They knew there was a price to pay for the good life, and it involved work.

However, this lazy man thought all the good things in life should come to him without any effort or involvement. Often he said to the villagers, "Why work if you can avoid it? I have lived my whole life wandering from place to place, asking people to take me in. They always feed me, often they give me clothes. Working is a fool's game!"

When he heard about the magical fig tree that had beautiful shades and succulent fruit throughout the year, he decided he should go and live beneath it. Why not? The fig tree did not belong to anyone, and he could spend his days eating the ripe fruit that fell from the branches.

He would not even need to climb the tree to collect fruit; he could lie beneath its branches with his mouth wide open and wait for the fruit to fall in. In his lazy mind, he imagined a happy life forever!

"Not only will I be fed throughout my life, I will also be able to look out over the beautiful forest, enjoy the fresh air, hear the birds sing, and admire the powerful mountains. See everyone? Good things really do come to you if are prepared to take advantage of them."

So for many months, Lazy Man lived and slept under the fig tree. Fruit would drop down and he would catch it in his mouth.

Because he was too lazy to move around, he would eat the fruit and just spit out any nasty parts. Occasionally, a fig would fall and hit him on the head or the birds would leave their droppings on him, but nothing really bothered him.

"When I think about all the advantages I have under this fig tree, why complain about the occasional bump on the head or a few bird droppings!"

People stopped coming to picnic at the fig tree because of the unsightliness of Lazy Man; besides, he was beginning to smell. It was a rare day indeed that he visited the stream for a wash. He saw nobody and nobody saw him.

It was interesting that nobody really sat down and tried to explain the severe limitations created by Lazy Man's existence!

Then one day, things began to change. As we all know, nothing remains the same. Sometimes unexpected happenings occur and our lives are changed. Life truly is a mystery.

On this day, Lazy Man was doing what he had always done for the past months, lying under the fig tree waiting for the juicy fruit to fall into his mouth. He had arranged himself into what he thought would be a good position. His mouth was open wide, but nothing happened.

He waited and waited, but still, nothing happened. He started to get hungry. Then he became irritated. He stretched his mouth to make it wider, but no fruit fell.

Now, he was becoming seriously hungry. He experienced hunger pangs he had never felt before.

He was away from the village, so he could not do what he had done all his life and beg for food. Now he was alone in the forest with the fig tree.

He became confused. He started to talk to himself. "What is happening up there? Hey, fruity fruit! Can you not see I am waiting for you? Do what you have always done. Fall into my mouth! See, here is my mouth, wide open. Come now little fruit, do not keep me waiting."

Then, to add insult to injury, a flock of birds that had never before appeared in such numbers, saw the juicy fruit on the fig tree and invited themselves to a succulent lunch. They were flying from the mountain area of Yep to take their summer vacation in the Han Thong area. Hundreds of birds enveloped the fig tree, pecking, poking, and eating the figs as they played with each other on the numerous branches. The birds could not resist the flavorsome fruit. Some did a little dance and a few created a song for the occasion.

We like to eat fruit
But we really love figs
It's a laxative we know
But it makes the journey lighter! Ha Ha.

Soon, the birds got a rhythm going and they sang this song for many minutes as they danced and jigged on the branches.

And the fruit really was a laxative for many of the birds so it was not long before Lazy Man was covered with bird droppings, but no fruit fell. It was a most joyous scene in the tree, but a horrible sight on the ground.

Lazy Man was a hungry mess. He stretched his mouth even wider, and nothing fell but the bird droppings.

"Yuck! Hey, move on you greedy birds! This is my tree. Stop singing that sickly song and get on your way."

The birds did not understand the language of Lazy Man, but they could not help but see the humor in the scene below. Now they all laughed, danced, and sang.

For the first time, Lazy Man began to think life was unfair. Eventually, the birds had enjoyed enough fun and they rested on the branches before continuing their journey to the vacation area at Han Thong.

Lazy Man was feeling awful. How could all this misery happen to him?

All his life he had been so free and easy, never worrying about anything; things had just come to him so effortlessly. He had never had to work, never had to fight for an easy, lazy life, but now everything was miserable.

He truly was confused. He did not know how to face life. Nothing was going the way he wanted. He began to cry. "I am so unhappy. So angry. I am so lonely. And really, really hungry. Why, why, why is life so unfair?"

For many hours he cried, occasionally beating the fig trunk with his hands. This only added to his pain because his hands blistered and eventually bled.

The birds all looked down from their branches at the sight of the crying lazy man in his tantrum. "Why does this man continue to lie beneath this tree, covered in dirt, droppings, and leaves, crying and feeling sorry for himself? All the people in the village are happy and joyous, whistling as they labor in their fields, talking with each other and planning their futures as their children play. This lazy man is creating his own sadness. He is a victim of his own helplessness!"

A holy man had been visiting the village and was journeying back to his monastery in the mountains, passing through the forest, when he heard the cries of Lazy Man. Moving in the direction of the fig tree, he saw the pitiful sight.

"Hey, Lazy Man, why are you crying?" Holy Man was naturally intuitive.

"Well, sir," Lazy Man could be very respectful when he wanted something.

"Well sir, I am very confused about my life at the moment. Things are not happening the way they should. Today is turning out so very differently from yesterday; indeed, today has taken a turn for the worse. I used to spend my days lying under the fig tree collecting the fruit in my mouth with no effort. But today, no fruit fell, and the birds came and had a party on the branches, eating all my fruit."

"*Your* fruit?" asked Holy Man.

"Yes, sir," replied Lazy Man.

"I do not think so. The fruit, the tree, the birds, and your life belong to God. Everything is a gift from God. We should all appreciate this principle in life.

"Let me tell you, my son, that life is to be experienced each day. And with life comes changes. You never know what is going to happen in any given day. This allows the smart people, I mean spiritually smart people, to be creative. We must deal with problems and challenges–that is how we grow. To be a positive and creative person, we must deal with life as it is, as it reveals itself–not how we want it to be.

"Life has many wonders, but they have to be discovered. Often, they are encountered through work. Work is a gift sent by God. Lazy people do not discover these wonders in life; lazy people do not discover the true mystery of God. With work and creativity comes joy. We enjoy life only when we are prepared to work at it. When problems arise in your life, you need to stand up, dust yourself off, and confront them.

"To overcome a challenge you must not be afraid to try. I fear you have been running away from life in the guise of your laziness. Now is the time to grow up."

The birds in the branches decided as a group to delay their trip to Han Thong so they could listen to Holy Man. Of course, they did not know what he was actually saying, but it sounded, and felt, important. Birds sense when something is sacred.

By now, Lazy Man had stopped crying and was listening intently to Holy Man.

"Now Lazy Man, I want you to stand up and come over to me. What I will show you is an important lesson in life." Holy Man walked to the trunk of the fig tree. Lazy Man, a little confused, followed Holy Man's instructions.

"Now with both hands on the trunk of the tree, I want you to push very hard; push and pull and shake the tree as hard as you can. Do not spare any effort. We are co-creating with God's energy to make what we want happen."

Lazy Man did what he was told. For many minutes, he pushed, pulled, and shook the trunk of the fig tree and soon, beautiful fruit fell from its branches.

The birds became a little dizzy for a moment but clapped their wings for joy and chirped loudly to show their admiration for Holy Man and their support for Lazy Man. After that, the birds decided the shaking tree was a sign for them to continue their journey. They did not want to waste any more vacation time in the forest!

Lazy Man was so happy. He began to gather up all the beautiful figs, placing them carefully in his pockets. He turned to thank Holy Man for such an important lesson in life, but Holy Man was gone. The Life Principle remained.

From that moment on, Lazy Man's thinking was changed. He decided to save some of the fruit until the next day. He would build himself a small hut and plant a fig tree to feed himself and then sell the leftovers in the village. Perhaps he would raise some chickens and pigs, maybe grow a vegetable garden.

In minutes, Lazy Man became excited about life and what he could do to produce his own happiness rather than depend upon others. He wanted to work. He wanted to join with God in creating for himself the "Good Life."

King Magpie
Vua Sáo

There once was a prosperous Kingdom, ruled by a middle-aged King and his aging wife, the Queen. The Queen was known throughout the land for being gentle and kindhearted.

They had only one daughter, the Princess, who was staggeringly beautiful. No language on Earth could fully describe her beauty.

Many of the people who were fortunate enough to see her were stunned by the radiance of her countenance and the elegance of her form. Some called her "the Goddess."

However, this undeniably beautiful Princess had a mean, self-centered personality and disposition. Not only did she irritate and upset the people who served her, it was said the very mountains and streams occasionally screamed at her attitude and behavior.

A holy monk was once heard to say, "She has a personality that angers God!"

Nothing was ever good enough for her. Food served was either too hot or too cold. A dress was either too long or too short. A drawn bath was always accompanied by argument: "This water is too perfumed or too hot or too cold. Where are the warm towels when I need them?"

You can imagine the stress the servants endured. Once, a harassed servant left a bar of soap on the floor near a marble washbowl.

The haughty Princess placed her foot on the soap and upended herself in a most unseemly manner; the servant was forced to eat rotten vegetables for a week. Mistakes were never tolerated in the spoiled world of the beautiful Princess.

Again, the holy monk was heard to remark, "A Princess who cannot tolerate human error is doomed to unhappiness and the slow death of spirit."

Nothing was ever good enough for her, and she lived to criticize. The best hairdresser in the land spent hours washing, combing, and trimming the Princess' hair; never did she appreciate the result. "This style makes me look like a scarecrow. Why does it stick up at the top? I am not a parrot!"

An acclaimed designer spent months designing dresses and gowns made from the finest silks and accompanied by the most decorous shawls and capes. "This dress makes me look too fat or too small or too dumpy. The colors do not enhance my natural beauty. Am I not a Princess? Why do you make me look like a farm girl?"

A famous chef from Burma, who once created a banquet for the King of France that lasted four days, could never please her sensitive palate. "Too spicy or too salty. Why do the vegetables all taste like cabbage?"

Most times she would put food in her mouth, then instantly spit it out. Large bowls were placed around her chair at each meal to collect the disgorged food. The palace dogs thought they were in heaven!

The most talented musical group in the Kingdom could not excite her passion. Often, she would walk out while they were still playing, murmuring "I have heard better harmony from a dying pigeon."

Nothing pleased her. She made misery popular.

Day after day, year after year, the King and his compassionate Queen, together with the royal household, had to endure the barrage of negativity from the undeniably beautiful Princess. Indeed, her beauty tended to confuse everybody and make them ambivalent because they could not understand how somebody so beautiful and elegant could be so cruel, selfish, and negative.

One day, the King and Queen engaged in a private conversation until the early hours of the morning. It was time to select a Prince for their daughter from the nearby region.

When they thought she was in a good mood, or, rather, a less crabby mood than usual, they called her into their private quarters in the palace. "Dearest and most beautiful daughter, the time has come for us to announce the day you will select a man of noble birth to be your husband. Your beauty and elegance is known throughout the Eastern world and Kings, Princes, and men of noble birth from far and wide will come and compete for your royal hand in marriage. However, it is important to us that you consider not just the imperial pedigree and wealth, but rather select a man who connects with the passion and love in your heart.

"Married bliss grows from a God-given energy we call romance *(tình yêu)*. We pray you find your soul mate chosen in heaven."

The announcement for the search of a noble husband was made in all the foreign lands for months before the special day arrived. All the villages in the Kingdom were decorated with flowers and colored taffeta, the roads were swept and cleaned, and even the animals were washed and combed for this most important occasion. Flags were flying from the portals of the castle and tapestries draped from the walls. The beauty everyone saw in the Princess was reflected in the beauty of the castle and outlying villages. Truly, the Kingdom had been changed into magnificence!

When the day came for the Princess to select her royal husband, the ceremony was highly orchestrated. The foreign notables were systematically lined up in order of age and imperial status.

The King and Queen were seated on a stage decorated with gold leaf and exotic flowers from each region of the Kingdom. The Princess was seated to the side of the King, attended by representatives from the Imperial Temple.

Strangely, because nobody quite knew how he got invited, the holy monk who had made such insightful comments concerning the personality of the Princess, was standing to the side of the High Priest. He was dressed in a simple Buddhist's habit, and holiness and wisdom shone from his eyes.

At the appropriate time, the royal suitors presented themselves before the King and Queen, offering precious stones, silver, and chests filled with gold bracelets and jeweled necklaces, together with government documents promising regional alliances. After each presentation, the King would turn to the Princess and ask, "Is he the one? Does he stir your heart? Do you think there is a possibility of a blissful romance blessed by God?"

The Princess replied, "No Father, he is too fat."

"No Father, he is too old."

"No Father, he has the face of a monkey."

"No Father, his breath smells of rotten eggs."

The holy monk spoke gently into the ear of the Princess. "Your Royal Highness, remember a man is more than his appearance. True beauty rests in the soul."

The Princess' response was quick and rude, "Shut up you silly monk. What can you possibly know about royal love! Attend to your prayers."

The monk serenely smiled.

Throughout the day, the Kings and Princes presented themselves, only to be rejected by the selfish, bad-tempered Princess. As sunset beckoned, the King stood up and turning to the people in the great square, the royal dignitaries who had come from far and wide, and the noble guests, he gently bowed.

He then did something strange that had not been arranged as part of the royal ceremony. With his head lowered, he walked and stood before the holy monk, then knelt and asked for a blessing:

"Holy Master, I ask your blessing for what I am about to proclaim. Your simple style of life clearly proclaims the glory of God and your wisdom is known throughout the land. I ask that what I speak reflects your prayers."

The King then turned to his daughter and proclaimed in a loud voice, "Dearest daughter, sweet Princess, my love for you is deeper than the sea and higher than the mountains. However, I can no longer tolerate your selfish, arrogant, and bad-tempered behavior that, like a sickness, has affected the royal household and the Kingdom. I have spoiled you from childhood, and I bear a heavy responsibility for the character and personality you have become.

"To everyone present, I announce my sincere apology. I decree that as the sun rises tomorrow, the first man who comes to the palace gate, rich or poor, young or old, handsome or ugly, he is the one you shall marry. So be it!"

The Princess was visibly shocked and frightened. She stood and trembled with anger. She turned sharply to the holy monk and sneered, "You have something to do with this. Your spirit entered my father. These words are not his."

The monk gently responded, "You told me to pray. Now you are discovering prayer is more powerful than all the wealth of every nation. Be careful what you ask for in God's world." He then fell silent.

During this time, there was beyond the mountains a handsome young King who was happy and loving to every man, woman, and child. He respected all the animals in his Kingdom and his gardens, growing and nurturing all manner of plants.

His eyes gleamed with contentment and rarely was he discovered without a gentle smile on his face. He was genuinely loved by his subjects and treated everyone with kindness and respect. He was nicknamed King Magpie.

He did not join the other Kings and Princes in seeking the hand of the Princess because he hated romantic competitions, especially trying to impress with wealth or political inducements. However, he had always loved the Princess from afar.

It so happened the holy monk, while returning to his temple in the northern region, visited King Magpie and told him what the old King had proclaimed before all the people: that the first person at the castle gate would receive the hand of his daughter–rich or poor.

The monk wisely observed, "The Princess has been spoiled by her father for many years and her true soul, gifted by God, has been encrusted with selfishness, pride, haughtiness, and arrogance. Undeniably, she is very beautiful, but her true beauty has never been revealed. God willing, her new husband will birth that beauty into the world."

"I shall be that husband," exclaimed King Magpie. "But I will not reveal my true self. I shall pretend to be a poor farmer, lost in a foreign land; I shall not seek to impress her with wealth and royal pedigree. I will win her heart with who I really am."

The holy monk discreetly smiled. He had always known the young King was the bad tempered Princess' true soul mate. Now that he had completed his mission, he took his leave from King Magpie and returned to his temple.

Before sunrise, King Magpie, dressed as a simple farmer, appeared at the castle gate. He was the first to arrive.

As the sun blinked over the mountains, he knocked at the big wooden doors. "I have come to claim the hand of the beautiful Princess."

When the old King saw him, he truly looked a sorry sight! Yet there was a noble presence the old King perceived in this young man. "I shall grant you your request. My beautiful daughter shall be your bride. Also, I shall offer you food and drink, together with a bag of gold so you can begin your new life together. May you discover the heavenly bliss only a true marriage can bring."

After they had eaten, the couple departed from the castle. The beautiful Princess turned and looked back at the magnificent castle that was no longer to be her home. And she quietly shed a tear.

They traveled for many days along the dusty paths, through forests and up and down hills, until they came to a tiny hut near a stream. It was in the middle of nowhere. King Magpie, still dressed as a simple farmer, turned to the Princess with his delightful smile and said in a gentle voice, "This will be our new home. I know it is not anything like what you are accustomed to, but I will do my best to make life good for us."

The Princess looked at the hut in horrified silence. A frown of disapproval was written across her face.

Hesitantly, she entered the hut and saw a simple table with an unlit candle, a few chairs, and a small bed in the corner. Dust was everywhere.

Never had she seen such a place. No servants. No mirrors. No flowers. In her mind, she thought she would die living here.

King Magpie whistled and smiled as he busied himself at the stove, cooking a few eggs and a little fish. The Princess just sat in stony silence.

He offered her some food. She refused with a brush of her hand.

Gently smiling, he said, "My dear wife, you will eat when you are hungry."

With that, he left her alone. He ate enthusiastically on his own, then went to sleep. The Princess just sat in stunned amazement.

The next day, King Magpie awoke early. The Princess was asleep on her little chair.

He decided to continue the pretense, washing his face in the stream and remaining in his farmer clothes. He busied himself building clay pots he would later sell in the village, paying no attention to the Princess.

Soon, the Princess became very hungry and thirsty. She could no longer just sit in the hut; she desperately needed to eat something. Walking into the forest, she began to pick wild mushrooms, which she brought back to the hut to cook.

Amazingly, the Princess was cooking for herself! And for the first time in her life, she shared her cooked mushrooms with King Magpie. He smiled in gratitude.

An entire year passed.

It was market day, and King Magpie, still pretending to be a simple farmer and potter, asked the Princess if she would go into the village and sell some pots. He would busy himself in the vegetable garden he had grown around the hut.

She went off to market, carrying a bag of heavy clay pots. She arranged them beautifully in delightful rows, but nobody bought anything. She returned feeling despondent and dejected.

King Magpie held her hands and gave her a gentle kiss on her cheek. "Do not feel sad. Tomorrow is another day. You will have a better day tomorrow."

The next day, she returned to market and again set up all her clay pots in delightful rows. However, King Magpie decided to play a little game with the Princess.

He secretly entered the village and, hiding from the Princess, he encouraged his horse to trot into her stall, breaking all her wares. Every single pot was broken.

The Princess was distraught and afraid to return home because everything was broken. She had nothing to sell.

Crying, she ran from the village and hid in the forest. King Magpie followed her and pretended to be looking all over for her.

When he eventually "discovered" her, she was still crying. "I am not good at anything," she told him. "I am not even a beautiful Princess. I am not a good wife. Look at me, I am ugly and useless."

King Magpie, smiling with gentle love, held her head between his hands and kissed her on both cheeks. "No, that is not true. You are the most beautiful woman in the whole world. I love you today more than ever. The clay pots may all be broken, but our hearts are healed. We are no longer separate. We have become one."

Putting her on his horse, he took her a mile through the forest. Eventually, they came to a beautiful castle, bigger and more magnificent than the one that belonged to her father and mother.

All the gardens were beautifully manicured and peacocks graced the lawns.

Still pretending, King Magpie asked, "Shall we knock on the gate and ask for some food and drink?" The Princess, ashamed of her appearance, begged him not to go near the castle, and certainly not to knock on the gate.

When they made their way toward the castle, the gates opened and all the people inside rushed toward them shouting with joy, "Welcome home, King Magpie! We have all missed you so much. How beautiful to see you with our new Queen."

The Princess almost fainted in amazement. For over a year, she had been living with King Magpie, thinking he was a lowly farmer and potter.

Now, she was a real Queen with a beauty that radiated from inside as well as out. A true beauty that glowed like the moon.

Standing by the gate, the old monk observed the transformation with a serene smile.

Best Friends
Đôi Bạn Thân

$\mathcal{M}$any years ago, there were two little boys: one named Thang and the other called Han. From a very young age, they always played together and were great friends. As they grew up, they attended the same school, studied hard together, and graduated with excellent experience in trading and export.

After graduation, it was not long before they both married, each one finding a gentle and beautiful wife. And yet even in marriage, as time consuming as it can surely be, they both continued to remain close friends, visiting each other and finding time to drink tea in the marketplace.

The neighbors saw them together and commented on how close they were; indeed, some said they were more thoughtful, loving, and caring now than when they were children.

It was not long before both Thang and Han became business owners, with much responsibility and tedious paperwork. However, they were still often seen organizing and managing laborers in adjoining fields, even though they worked for different owners that were headquartered in separate towns.

Everyone in the vicinity could hear them laughing together and calling sweet messages, sharing ideas, and offering advice for business improvements, new ventures, and just about everything. Both became very successful. They were the best of friends.

Life, as we know, is not always smooth sailing, and one day, tragedy struck. Thang's head office and adjoining buildings burned down and all his venture capital, business materials, and possessions were ashes. Apparently, a drunken laborer had thrown a lit cigarette in a dry rice field as he absentmindedly observed a pretty girl pass by on her bicycle. Innocence often precedes tragedy.

Thang and his wife were devastated and financially ruined by the fire. After much heartache and debate, they decided to visit Han and ask if they could work for him in the fields.

Han genuinely loved his friend and would not hear of Thang and his wife working in the fields as mere laborers; rather, he intended to give a substantial loan to Thang so he could reinvest in his business and build up the company that had burned down. For years, Han had put a percentage of money each month into a "rainy day" fund, knowing nobody really knows what fate awaits us in life.

Han was joyously happy to share his nest egg with his best friend and was about to retrieve the gold from his secret hiding place when Thang told him to listen to what he had to say.

"My best friend, please come sit and hear what I must tell you. I know you love me dearly and care for my family and business, but I do not want your loan. I know it comes from the kindness of your generous heart, but I fear my bad luck has not yet gone away. Let me just work for you in the fields as a laborer for a while, and when I feel this bad luck has gone, then we can reconsider your offer. But not now, I beg you."

Han and his wife reluctantly agreed and hired Thang and his wife to work for them, valuing their friendship and offering them unconditional love.

The results were incredible. Thang had great talent and trading experience. He was clever at connecting with others and his God-given friendly attitude was rooted in a deep respect for all the clients.

Within three years, Thang helped Han's business to grow five times in size from when he started working for him. Han was soon becoming the richest man in the Northern Kingdom.

One day, Han shouted to Thang to come out from his little office and drink tea as they had done years ago when they were young men.

"My dear Thang, you have been such a loyal and hard worker. Every day from morning to night, you work in the fields, managing the people who work hard for me, each year making me a profit of over 400%.

"Even your dear wife is working hard for me in the fields. Now is the time for your reward. Surely your bad luck has gone away by now. It is time for you to take 50 percent, yes, I really mean 50 percent, of all you have created and return to your own town and slowly begin to build up your own business. There is surely room in the trading and export business for both of us."

Thang was deeply touched by his friend's love, loyalty, and support and accepted the gift with happy tears in his eyes. Even his wife, who stood outside the door listening, cried happy tears.

Things had gone very well for Han and his wife for many years. From the time he was a young man, he had worked hard and put "rainy day" money away.

Indeed, Han was one of the richest men in the Northern Kingdom, but destiny sometimes creates strange energy.

For a year or more, although his business had been doing very well, Han had surrounded himself with dissolute and lazy friends. Han's wife called them leeches and maggots, living off Han's wealth and prosperity.

Every neighborhood and town has its disreputable characters, and for years, Han had avoided them. But now, they had squirreled into his business and social life.

After work, he went to the bars and gambling houses instead of returning home to his wife for a nice meal, staying out all night, then going into work the next day tired and drowsy. His wife became concerned about Han's crazy and irresponsible lifestyle and begged him to return to his former ways.

But Han was too proud and would not listen. Indeed, he threw uncooked vegetables at her, screaming, "Stay in the kitchen, woman, where you belong!"

Han's wife lowered her head and cried in the corner for days. Her tears flowed like a river.

Every month, week, and day, the profits from the business began to shrink. Things were not good.

Han's gambling and drinking increased. The leeches and maggots multiplied. Soon he was in debt. The situation got so bad that Han sat next to his wife in the corner where she was crying and told her he was going away because he was not a good husband.

He would visit his old friend Thang. He would ask Thang for help. Remember, Thang was his best friend.

It had been so long since Thang had seen Han. Thang was so happy to see his friend again. Thang's wife prepared a banquet feast of roast pig, fish, duck, and pomegranates.

Over dinner, Han shared his news and told Thang of the bad luck that had now visited him. He was in debt. He had a wife that constantly cried in the corner of their house. He had no true friends in the town.

"Only you, my best friend, can I come to for help!"

Thang listened to his friend. He observed the effects of prolonged drinking and gambling on Han's body and emotions.

He was reluctant to offer Han any money, fearing it would only be squandered away on drinking and gambling. What should he do?

Thang came up with an idea that he hoped his friend would appreciate. He would not give Han money, but he would make him a manager in his business.

Each day, from morning to evening, he would encourage Han to live a sober and responsible life, knowing that in the future he would be able to return to his wife and business.

Some people in the town were critical of Thang because they remembered how Han had helped him when the fire had destroyed his business years ago, but Thang trusted his instincts and wanted only what was good for his best friend.

However, Thang did a secret thing. Without telling Han, Thang determined to send Han's wife a sum of money to assist her through the months and also help Han's business to grow–but he pretended the money was being sent by Han.

The money and directions for its use were clear: Pay off the debts, take care of herself, and build up the business.

Each month, the money was sent to Han's wife as regular as an efficient clock, and each month, Han's wife cried happy tears, believing Han was getting his life together. Over time, Han's business slowly improved.

Han's wife worked very hard, as she had done all through their married life, because she was so grateful for the money Han was sending her each month. Like most loving wives, she did not want to disappoint her husband.

Of course, she did not know the secret: it was Thang, Han's best friend, who was sending the money each month.

One day, Han's wife decided to write a letter back to her husband to say the business was doing extremely well and it was time for him to say goodbye to Thang and return to her. It was time for him, she said, to return and take responsibility for the business.

However, the letter from Han's wife was intercepted by Thang, who had been sending money to her each month and he did not want Han to know, certainly not at the present time, that all was going well with his business in the other town. Thang was afraid that Han was not really ready to face his responsibilities; indeed he was still a long way from having a clear insight into his irresponsible behavior.

Although Han was working very hard for Thang in the daytime, he was still meeting up with his dissolute friends in the evening, spending what little money he had on drinking and gambling!

However, Thang was Han's best friend and whenever he could find time, he would spend it with Han, talking about the need to stay sober, be personally responsible for his own money, stay healthy by eating properly, and getting sustained rest. Thang also made sure that Han, along with his other bad habits, had not gotten into dishonesty and theft. Thank God Han, who was undoubtedly irresponsible, had not become a financial crook!

Although Han was still being dissolute in the evening, in the company of the leeches and maggots, he was working hard during the day for Thang. Thang's business prospered.

Indeed, he was soon ready to open another warehouse in another part of town. He decided to take a risk and ask Han to be the manager for the new business, hoping that if he was busy with more responsibility, he would find less time for evening escapades in the bars and gambling houses.

Maybe, just maybe, that magic moment of spiritual harmony would emerge and create the all-important character change.

Well, miracles never cease to happen if you are persistent. Han threw himself into managing the new business, working day and night for Thang, and soon, he had little energy for going out in the evening with his dissolute friends. In the evening, after a good dinner of rice and pork, or sometimes vegetables and fish, he rested, going to bed early and embracing a peaceful sleep.

As time went by, Han completely separated himself from the people and events that had so nearly destroyed his life and marriage. His new pleasure was found in dreaming of the day he would return to his wife, build up the business that had all but been destroyed, saving up his wages for this noble enterprise.

Often, his heart was sad, and he regretted terribly the wasted years when he had gambled and drunk away the fortune, causing his wife to cry in the corner.

One morning, Han arose early and walked to meet his best friend Thang for tea in the marketplace as they had done so many years before, and this time he carried with him a bag of gold coins.

"Best friend Thang, I am indebted to the many years of friendship we have shared together. You indeed have been my best friend. Since I have been working for you, I have not really considered my dear wife and the business I left behind so many years ago. I feel so ashamed. Today, I know I am guilty of a dissolute lifestyle, throwing money away in drinking and gambling, destroying a family life, being an irresponsible man. However, I want to right my wrongs. Some months ago, I started saving money for my beautiful wife and business. Although it is not much, it is the result of honest sweat and labor. I have learned the value and potential of hard work. I treasure it so much. Please, my best friend, take this bag of gold and give it to my dear wife so she can use it to settle any debts and join me here with you. Together we will be a family."

Thang lovingly smiled at his friend Han. They had always been best friends, and he always knew his friend carried a true heart.

"Dear Han, I have been waiting for this day for a long, long time. If you wish to send for your wife to join you here with me, that would be no problem. I am sure she is awaiting your messages. However, I have a better idea. Why don't you go and visit her, take your bag of gold coins, and I will give you extra money for your travels to the next town. Your wife is surely missing you, Han, and I know she will be so very excited to see you again. Remember, we are forever the best of friends. What is yours is mine and what is mine is yours."

Han thanked his friend and nervously began his travels to the next town to see his wife after many years. Although he was anxious, there was also a part of him that was both excited and happy.

It was a strange feeling to walk the cobbled streets of his town, see old neighbors, and pass by the teahouse where he had taken refreshment after Thang's business burned down so many years ago.

He tried hard to locate his building, but was afraid to ask directions. He stood in the middle of the street, looking peacefully confused. He was lost, but home.

Then scary thoughts crept into his head. "Maybe when I was poor and in so much debt, my wife sold the business. Maybe she went through terrible times of hardship and married again. Maybe . . ."

Depressing thoughts were spinning around his head, touching his soul, and then he found himself standing in front of a busy merchant's house. Customers were rushing in and out, and prosperity oozed from the business.

Then, in an instant, he saw his wife; almost at the same time, she looked up from her paperwork and their eyes gently met. For a few seconds, she stared in disbelief. "Is this my husband?" She thought. "Yes, it is, it really is," and she yelled with excitement.

"Han is home! Everyone look! Han has returned. He has come. My loving husband has returned!"

And a young child stood by his mother's side. He looked just like Han. Han had a son.

Over the week that followed, Han's wife told him about the money that had been sent regularly each month. Tears welled up in Han's eyes because he knew the money had been sent by Thang. His heart was filled with love for his friend and he felt a gratitude that could never be fully expressed by words or deeds.

Han treasured Thang's friendship. It was truly a demonstration of best friends–a friendship that would endure to the end of time.

About the Author

Dynamic, challenging, insightful, and witty, Father Leo Booth is a priest cut from a different cloth. He claims you do not have to be religious to be spiritual and is as likely to quote from the Beatles, *The Velveteen Rabbit,* or Oscar Wilde, as he is from the Bible. His passion is to help us discover God and spirituality are not "out there" somewhere, but are found within ourselves and our world.

Father Leo is an internationally acclaimed author, lecturer, and trainer on all aspects of spirituality and recovery including depression, addictions, compulsive behaviors, and low self-esteem. He holds a Masters degree in Theology from King's College, London, England, is a Certified Addictions Counselor and Certified Eating Disorders Counselor, and a national consultant to hospitals and psychiatric centers. In addition, Father Leo presents workshops, lectures, and training on a broad spectrum of issues, to a variety of organizations and institutions. He is a contributing columnist to several publications. Father Leo has appeared on television shows such as *Oprah Winfrey, Geraldo, Sally Jesse Raphael,* and others.

Father Leo was born in England and raised in a home divided by religious arguments. Driven and ambitious, he became one of the youngest rectors in England. Since a drunken car crash in 1977 led to his treatment for alcoholism, he has devoted his work to helping addicts and others who suffer from low self-esteem. From his work as both priest and addictions counselor, he has developed a new spiritual model based on Choice, Action, Responsibility, and Empowerment.

Catalogue

Books by Father Leo

When God Becomes a Drug
A challenging and insightful look at the symptoms and sources of religious addiction and abuse is also a guide to attaining healthy spirituality. It offers tools for recovery from religious abuse, as well as a guide for therapists and step-by-step guide to intervention. *(SCP Limited $15.00)*

The God Game: It's Your Move
Father Leo's daring book answers the oft-asked question, "Why can't I get spiritual?" The answer, he says, is that we already are. But the messages and experiences we've had since childhood form a God-Box that stops our ability to truly activate new spiritual concepts. *The God Game* explores moving from spiritual pawn to powerful player with God in the adventure of life. *(SCP Limited $15.00)*

Say Yes to Life: Continuing the Journey
A ten-week workbook for developing spirituality, recovery, and healing. *(SCP Limited $35.00)*

The Angel and the Frog
In this charming spiritual fable, Cedric the frog and the residents of Olde Stable Farm meet an angel named Christine and discover the Spiritual Process. *(SCP Limited $12.95)*

Spirituality and Recovery
One of Father Leo's most popular works, this book is a guide to creating healthy spirituality in recovery. It explains the difference between religion and spirituality, and suggests ways in which to become a more positive, creative person. *(SCP Limited $10.00)*

Meditations for Compulsive People

Father Leo brings his celebrated wit and insight to these unusual meditations on finding God in the odd and ordinary places of life. From cake to computers, gambling to Oscar Wilde, boogeymen to baked beans and his dog Winston, Father Leo shows all the different ways and places to strengthen our partnership with God. Each meditation is followed by process questions to help guide you to a new way to relate to God, yourself and the world around you. *(SCP Limited $10.00)*

The Wisdom of Letting Go: The Path of the Wounded Soul

This book was inspired by the numerous workshops Father Leo did across the country. People from all walks of life asked the same basic question: "How do I let go?" This book seeks to be the answer. *(SCP Limited $15.00)*

Say Yes to Life Daily Meditations

These 365 daily meditations on issues relating to alcoholism, chemical dependency, eating disorders, and codependency provide the best of Father Leo. They are thoughtful, challenging, and humorous, and offer hope for recovery. *(SCP Limited $10.00)*

Treasures: Awakening Our Spiritual Gifts

Spirit can be found in the ordinary happenings of life: rides in taxicabs, lines at the airport, and Rudolph the Red-Nosed Reindeer. Father Leo takes you on an extraordinary journey to find Spirit in what appear to be ordinary events. *Treasures* celebrates the awareness of God in places few people are likely to perceive God. *(SCP Limited $15.00)*

Audios by Father Leo

Audio Albums $28.00 each

- Say Yes To Life (A1,B4,B5,C6)
- Overcoming Religious Addiction & Religious Abuse
  (B1,B3,B6,C4)
- Using the Celestine Principles (D6,E1,E2,E3)
- Creating Healthy Relationships (A3,A5,B2,C5)
- Masterminding for the New Millenium
- Awakening Our Spirituality
- Turning Obstacles Into Opportunities
- Insight, Wisdom & Harmony
  (Based on *The Angel & The Frog*)

Or create your own album; choose any four individual audio tapes and receive all four at the special album price along with an attractive case. Individual Audio Tapes $10.00 each:

A1 Say Yes To Life
A2 The Twelve Step Lifestyle
A3 Spirituality & Adult Child Recovery
A4 My Life Story
A5 Surrender Brings Sanity
A6 Intervention: Creating an Opportunity to Live
B1 Recovery From an Eating Disorder
B2 Addiction: Effect Upon the Family
B3 Overcoming Guilt and Shame
B4 Relapse: A Spiritual Breakdown
B5 Positive Attitudes in Recovery
B6 Sexuality and Recovery

C1 Meditations for Compulsive People
C2 Say Yes to Relationships
C3 Overcoming Depression
C4 Overcoming Religious Abuse
C5 Creating Healthy Relationships
C6 Overcoming Resentments
C7 Codependency: Learning to Love
C8 Recovery From the Lie: Cocaine
D1 Creating Healthy Relationships: Know Your Boundaries
D2 It's Not What You're Eating
D3 When Money Doesn't Fix It
D4 Self-Esteem: How to Achieve It
D5 Learning to Overcome Stress

Videos by Father Leo

VHS 55 Mins $75.00 each

V1 Say Yes To Life
V2 Meditations for Compulsive People
V3 Spirituality and Adult Child Recovery
V4 Creating Healthy Relationships
V5 Recovery From an Eating Disorder
V6 Intervention: Creating an Opportunity to Live
V7 Overcoming Religious Addiction & Religious Abuse
V8 An Evening With Father Leo

Annual Spiritual Empowerment Conference Cruises & Retreats

Each year, Father Leo presents spiritual empowerment vacations and retreats. During these fun-filled days, you explore healthy spirituality, from the morning "Attitude of Gratitude" to the evening entertainment. Each event's theme focuses on some aspect of recovery from low self-esteem and addictions. Early reservations are recommended. Call Spiritual Concepts for current details.

Conferences · Workshops · Inservices · Consultancies

Father Leo works with a variety of groups and organizations from treatment centers and therapists to the general public teaching how to create healthy spirituality. The Spiritual Concepts staff can help you with any phase of the event, from choosing a topic to suggesting marketing strategies and creating ads and flyers for your event. If you would like to share Father Leo's wit and wisdom with your program or organization, call Spiritual Concepts.

For more information, or to place an order, call

Spiritual Concepts

(800) 284-2804

(8:00 AM – 4:00 PM Pacific time Monday-Friday)
2105 East 27th Street
Signal Hill, CA 90755
Internet: www.fatherleo.com
Email: fatherleo@fatherleo.com

Healing Thoughts
by Father Leo

Today is not a good day.
The news is depressing.

Friends seem absent...
I am alone

But I am alive.

I have the precious gift
of freedom.

The choice to smile is
still mine

We find joy
when we discover
the art of living
a grateful life

Once I am able to accept
my humanness,
then the burdens
or unrealistic
expectations
are removed.

Love is
feeling free enough
to express yourself
imperfectly.

Love is discovering the beauty
in the beast.

Tough love is recognizing the
beast in the beauty.

Why do I find it so hard to
forgive some people?

Because they reveal some
aspects of me that I don't want
to see.

Forgiveness requires
rigorous honesty.

The ability to forgive is a
precious gift.

Without forgiveness there could
be no relationships.

For those with
eyes to see,
everything that exists
pertains to Spirituality.